CW00762250

or before
low.

CAMBRIDGESHIRE

Edited by Lynsey Hawkins

First published in Great Britain in 2002 by
YOUNG WRITERS
Remus House,
Coltsfoot Drive,
Peterborough, PE2 9JX
Telephone (01733) 890066

HB ISBN 0 75433 970 X
SB ISBN 0 75433 971 8

FOREWORD

This year, Young Writers proudly presents a showcase of the best short stories and creative writing from today's up-and-coming writers.

We set the challenge of writing for one of our four themes - 'General Short Stories', 'Ghost Stories', 'Tales With A Twist' and 'A Day In The Life Of . . .'. The effort and imagination expressed by each individual writer was more than impressive and made selecting entries an enjoyable, yet demanding, task.

Write On! Cambridgeshire is a collection that we feel you are sure to enjoy - featuring the very best young authors of the future. Their hard work and enthusiasm clearly shines within these pages, highlighting the achievement each story represents.

We hope you are as pleased with the final selection as we are and that you will continue to enjoy this special collection for many years to come.

CONTENTS

Barton School

Kavita Babbar	1
Kate Seymour	2
Rosie Brock	4
Richard Gladders	6
Lucas Lilja	7
Alastair Smith	8
Hannah Nelms	9
Emma Hall	10
Bryony Craig-Matthews	11
Chris Davies	12
Mark Day	13
Elspeth Gibbs	14
Sophie Harding	15
Laura Packman	16
Catherine McLaughlin	17
Chris Hardwick	18
Josh Wright	19

Earith Primary School

Stephanie Freeman	20
Kasia Kaluza-Gilbert	22
Max Hutchins	23
Emma Sewell	24
Aaron Andrus	25
Nicole McGarrey	26
Hannah Wilson	27
Bethan Pritchard	28
Shaun Smith	29
Daryl Smith	30
Andrew Watson	31
Emma-Louise Hetherington	32
David Newman	33
Helen Mallett	34

Daniel Bainbridge 36
Dylan Dearnaley 38
Johnathan Griffiths 40

Stanground St John's School
Karleen Briggs 42
Christopher Morton 43
Hayley Boyden 44
Holli Mayo 45

Welland Primary School
James Liddell 46
Daniel Martin 47
Katie Thorogood 48
Adam Jackson 49
Leoni Moseley 50
Thomas McGlynn 51
Carl Pate 52
Alex Bedford 53

Westfield Junior School
Jodie McLaren 54
Jack Marshall 55
Usman Ali 56
Benjamin Chaffe 57
Hayley Cannon 58
Daniel Mountain-Chambers 59
Emily McGregor 60
William Winson-Pearce 61
Josh John 62
Hannah Mills 63
Christopher Unwin 64
Aaron Cohen-Gold 65
Kiri Storey 66
Sophie Wood 67
Chloe Andrews 68
Sophie Banks 69

Samantha Ambler	70
Emily-Jane Sparks	71
Jenna Spencer-Briggs	72
Jemma Yeowart	73
Lucy Jones	74
Ruby Pratt	75
Chloe Ackerlay	76
Samuel Weston	77
Stacey Fletcher	78
Chantelle Keepin	79
Peter Cox	80
Luke Bird	81
George Purvis	82
Kurt Noack	83
Sammy Kay	84
Aydn Reece	85
Charlotte Hood	86
Santino Zicchi	87
Courtney Woodrow	88
Jade Hannah	89
Henna Hussain	90
Rajane Kaur	91
Sarah Luxon	92
Sophie Raine	93
Adam Cash	94
Joel Marshall	95
Liam Parker	96
Lisette Cook	97
Jacob Hawkins	98
Hannah Dale	99
Giuseppe Polvere	100
Matthew Davis	101
Alphie Burgess	102
Charlotte Goodwin	103
Sarah Kinder	104
Ryan Hornett	105
Catherine Pritchard	106

Rowan Staden   107
Amelia Briggs   108
Paul Long   109
Tom Howard   110

The Stories

THE PEBBLE

The pebble caught my eye instantly as I wandered along the beach, I picked it up. It felt strangely warm in my hand. I heard something, it was coming from the pebble. It told me to make a wish. Well, I heard it again and then it repeated, 'Make a wish.' I didn't really know what to do because it was a very faint voice. I dashed away to get some food. I needed an ice lolly, but the ice cream van was not there, so I held the pebble in my hand and made a wish.

'I wish the ice cream van was here.' To my amazement, it was beeping along and came right near me. I started to think that it was a lucky pebble.

I ran back to my mum and it was time to go, but the problem was that I always felt car sick when I travelled in the car. I waited for mum and dad to pack up, we made our way to Wales where we were going to stay for the whole two weeks. I went to my room and studied the pebble. It was colourful, like green gems. I made another wish, and momentarily I was in England. I wished myself back to the hotel and suddenly, I was back at the hotel.

I was in a whole land of wishes! I ran to the living room. My mum said, 'I wish I had a cot for Jaiya,' and the wish was granted. The doorbell rang and the cot was delivered to the door.

One week later, we went back to the beach and played. While Mum and Dad had a rest on beach. Jaiya played with me and I sat her down on the smooth sand. I made lots of wishes and I thought the pebble went out of my hands and things came flying towards the beach. I threw the pebble in the water. It was all over, but my dream was no longer in my hands, it was travelling north. I estimated how long it would take to get somewhere. I guessed it would take two weeks and two weeks later it was found by . . .

Kavita Babbar (9)
Barton School

A Day In The Life Of A Race Horse

I woke up one morning to find that I had fallen asleep standing up, but then I realised I had four long furry legs with funny feet and a long neck. By that time I was scared, so I decided to have a look around to see where I was. I took a few steps and it sounded like horse's hooves. Then it struck me, I was a horse!

Now I had found out what I was, I was not so frightened, but just to make sure I was a horse, I decided to see what I sounded like. I took a deep breath and screamed, but it came out like 'nhaay!'

A few minutes later, I heard someone running towards me. It was a man. He was quite tall and had black hair. He came up to my stable and called out, 'Sparky.' I guessed it was me, so I went over. He gave me a little pat on my neck and walked into the room next to me. Then he came out again with a bowl of something and dropped it over my stable door. I went over to the bowl and sniffed it. It smelt quite nice so I decided to try some and I ate a little bit. It tasted quite nice, it was like a big mixture of food because it had sweet stuff, dry and chewy food.

When I had finished, I heard a big vehicle coming towards my direction. It was a big green lorry. Another man climbed out of the lorry and walked towards me. He opened the wooden door to my stable, came in, took a collar off the wall and put it around my head. He led me out of the stable, onto some concrete and tied me up. Another man came running down the path, then the two men started talking. They undid the door on the back of the lorry then one of them ran over to me, untied me and put me in the lorry. The other man got a box of brushes and two pieces of tack. One piece looked like the thing that would go over my head, which must be a bridle, and the other piece must be a saddle which goes on my back. As they closed the door, the engine started and then I was off somewhere.

When the lorry stopped I could hear talking, then two men opened the door and led me out of the lorry. The only difference was I was somewhere strange and one of the men was in purple and white. He was also wearing a hat. I was at a horse race.

About ten minutes later I was being tacked up. The saddle was quite heavy, but the bridle was not so bad. Suddenly, I was being mounted by the man in purple and white and then he kicked me. I started to walk. The next minute, I found myself at the starting line. Suddenly a big, booming voice shouted, 'On your marks, get set, go!'

I started running with all my might. I came to a fence, I jumped it. I came to another, I jumped that too. After about ten minutes of continuous running, I could see the finish. I was in the lead. I crossed the finish line, I had won.

Later, I received a cup and the biggest rosette I'd ever seen. After that, we went straight home. It's quite an exciting life being a race horse.

Kate Seymour (9)
Barton School

THE PEBBLE

The pebble caught my eye instantly as I wandered along the beach. I picked it up. It felt strangely warm in my hand. I turned it over to see that it had been cut in half. It felt smooth and shiny compared to the other side which was bumpy and rough. There were red rubies glinting in the sunlight. It looked like it had been sprinkled with emerald green glitter as well.

There was still some sand on the amazing pebble, so I rubbed it off. To my amazement, a genie floated out of the top. He was wearing lightish green trousers with a shirt to match. He had a white turban with a sapphire set in gold on it. He was no bigger than two inches tall. He told me in a deep, growling voice that I could have three wishes, so I said, 'I wish I could be famous.'
Immediately I was whirling round and round, higher and higher! Suddenly, I was sitting in what I think was a dark prison cell. There was a crack in the ceiling where water was leaking through and dripping onto the grimy floor. Desperate to know who I was, I leapt up and looked into the growing puddle. I knew that I had seen that face before, it had been on the news. I was the bank robber who had just been caught. I was Sally Gates. I suppose I was famous, but not in the way that I wanted.

The pebble was still in my hand. I rubbed it and the genie popped out. I wished that I could be someone famous that everyone likes! I heard the whooshing noise again. Right away, I was sitting in a comfy chair with my leg in plaster resting on a posh, glass coffee table. It took me a few seconds to realise I was David Beckham, so I shouted, 'Victoria! Can I have something to eat?' She came in with a carrot! 'Is there anything else?' I asked.
'You can have an apple, but you know what the doctor said. Carrots and apples only.'

I rubbed the pebble and the genie reminded me that I only had one wish left, but I said, 'I want to be me again.'
I was back on the beach with only one thought in my head, never pick up a pebble again!

Rosie Brock (11)
Barton School

THE PEBBLE

The pebble caught my eye instantly as I wandered along the beach. I picked it up. It felt strangely warm in my hand. I realised it was warm because it had been in the sun all day, but it looked nice, so I took it home as a souvenir.

When I got home, I cleaned all the sand off. To my amazement it was glass. I rubbed a mark off the pebble. Suddenly words came up, like credits at the end of a film. It read, 'Hello, what can I do for you, give me a question?'
So I replied, 'Fine, tell me tomorrow's headline.'
'Tomorrow, a skyscraper will fall in New York and many innocent people will die.'
I thought, yeah right and forgot about it. The next day when I got home from school, my mum was in tears. She pointed towards the TV, the Twin Towers had fallen down because of a terrorist attack. I remembered what the pebble told me. I went to my room to where it was, but when I got there, it had turned to sand. I threw the sand in the bin.

The next day as I walked to school, the garbage truck (with my sand in) had broken down. I'll never know if it was by chance or if the pebble was unlucky, but at least it is gone forever.

Richard Gladders (11)
Barton School

THE PEBBLE

The pebble caught my eye instantly as I wandered along the beach. I picked it up. It felt strangely warm in my hand. Suddenly, I teleported to a dragon world. I started to turn into a dragon, then I realised that this was a computer game. I had to find gems and eggs. The pebble was worth thousands of gems, so I saved it, then I found an egg.

I teleported back to the dragon world. I saw a rhino with armour, so I charged at him. I got five gems for killing him. I saw a salesman holding a kangaroo, called Sheila, behind bars. I said, 'I will buy that kangaroo for three hundred gems.'
Then he sang, 'Yes, yes, yes. I simply love gems!'

I entered Sheila's world and I helped Sheila kill all the rhinos. I found two eggs and a heap of guns. I also found a fairy and I learnt how to flame-throw. First I sneezed, some sparks came out, the second time a flame came out. The rhinos had built a small village, so I had to flame and charge at them to break their huts. Sheila helped by punching.

My friend the cheetah, called Hunter, got stolen and taken to the molten crater, so I went to the molten crater desperately searching for Hunter. I saw loads of rhinos, so I shut my eyes and charged through the small rhinos. I found one egg. I saw some huge rhinos which I had to flame, but they started throwing barrels which I had to dodge, then I flamed them! I found Hunter, but there was a huge rhino. She was the boss. She was wearing golden armour and had dynamite in her belt. I flamed her, but she threw some dynamite and it hurt me, then she ran away! Hunter gave me an egg.

Suddenly, I teleported home and a letter said, 'You are welcome back at any time.'

Lucas Lilja (10)
Barton School

THE PEBBLE

The pebble caught my eye instantly as I wandered along the beach. I picked it up, it felt strangely warm in my hands . . . The sea is cold on my feet, but my pebble's so warm. The Florida sun burns on my neck and hands. It's the biggest grey pebble I've ever seen. It's smooth and shiny. I look for a friend to show.

'Sniffy,' I heard Mike, another homeless boy call out as I sniffed loudly.

'Look what I found!' I exclaimed.

'That looks like a piece of jewellery,' said Mike.

Mike takes us to the harbour to meet his friend, Mr Cay. Mr Cay takes us aboard his boat. He kills Mike and ties me up. 'Where did you find that stone?' shouted Mr cay as he held a dagger to my face. 'Tell me!' he grunted.

I was too scared to have a voice, I could say nothing, but I managed to release my legs and kick the knife from his hand. Mr Cay fell into the water. I was still tied up, but I managed to steer the boat back to port where the police were waiting for me. They untied me and I showed them the stone. They had been looking for it. The stone was a piece of jewellery that had been stolen by Mr Cay, but he had lost it. I showed the police where I'd found it, there were sackfuls of jewels. Although Mr Cay was dead, the rest of his gang were locked up and I was rewarded, which meant I could sleep in a warm bed at night.

Alastair Smith (10)
Barton School

THE PEBBLE

The year was 2005 and I was on the beach when suddenly I spotted a glowing pebble. As I picked it up, I spotted two more. As I picked them up, suddenly there was a flash . . .

When I looked up, I was in a weird place. It was a big room and there was a man facing me. He was about two metres tall and looked exactly like a character from my favourite game, Powerstone. It was Valgas. I jumped up, realising I was dressed in a pink shirt and matching skirt.

Then the fight began. I grabbed a powerstone, then kicked him. Then I grabbed the last powerstone and transformed. I suddenly knew what to do, I leapt forward hitting him in a flurry of electrical flips and kicks. Valgas was down, it was a powerfusion move.

Then I saw my brother. As I ran forward to defeat him, there was a flash. I was back on the beach. One thought was in my mind. *Never go to the beach again!*

Hannah Nelms (10)
Barton School

A Day In The Life Of A Tiger

I woke up. My mother had left me. I now had to become an adult. I am a tiger. My whiskers are long, my coat is shiny with bright orange. She, my mother, had taught me everything I needed to know. I was hungry, so I needed to hunt.

I knew where the antelope were. They would be a fine breakfast. Slowly I crept to where the herd ate. I saw a young antelope, an easy meal. I did what my mother had told me. I pounced. I purred while eating the young antelope. Now I needed a home to sleep in.

I had found the perfect place. It was safe and well hidden in the safety of the trees. The shade now cooled me down. I had a nap. My sleep was peaceful. Suddenly, a *bang* woke me up. 'Guns!' I growled to myself. I went to see. They were poachers! They had an evil look in their eyes. I knew them. One had killed my brother, so I led them to a dead end and then snuck away. I was sure they would never find me again. They were now deep in the jungle and were lost. I heard them running in different directions.

Today, I learnt how to hunt and live safely. I went to my new home and fell asleep.

Emma Hall (10)
Barton School

THE PEBBLE

The pebble caught my eye instantly as I wandered along the beach. I picked it up. It felt strangely warm in my hand. Suddenly, the pebble turned into a tiny wee man. He had a sword, a shield, a bow and arrows. He was wearing a little tunic. He seemed to be very scared of me, but after a minute he sat on my hand. He started telling me how he became a pebble.

He whispered, when he was a little boy, a witch put a curse on him so that when he grew up he would turn into stone. When his wife touched him, he turned into a pebble. His wife and children turned into pebbles as well. They all got transported to the beach.
'When you picked me up, I turned into a man, but very small.'
He finished telling me the story then asked me to help his family. I touched three more pebbles, one of them turned into a woman. The other two turned into a little boy and girl. They thanked me and touched another stone. I got transported back to the same beach, exactly where I had started. The small family were nowhere to be seen. No one ever saw the little people on the beach, but people have claimed to have seen little people playing in the sea and on the sand . . .

Bryony Craig-Matthews (9)
Barton School

A Day In The Life Of Duke Nukem

One day, I went downstairs on a normal Saturday morning and turned on the PlayStation. I rubbed the sleepy dust out of my eyes so I could see properly. Then I saw a cave right in front of me and a bear staggering towards me
I yelled, 'How did that bear get in my house!'
It roared an angry roar.

I grabbed a machete that was next to me. I stabbed the bear, it fell to the ground, lifeless. I looked at myself, I wasn't me, I was a computer game character. All I can do now I suppose, is to complete the game. I looked around for a gun or weapon. I picked up an AK47, at least that's what the little screen said it was!

I ran into the cave. I realised that I could jump higher than a normal man. I came up to a corner thinking I could beat everything, but after that I changed my mind. A huge thing that screamed was in front of me. I shot it while sidestepping so the blows of the thing would not affect me. It hit me, I was forced backwards. Eventually, I killed it.
'Level One complete,' said a voice. 'Next level loading.'

I walked into an arena. The door slammed behind me and a huge lizard walked in. I picked up a shotgun, put a cartridge in and shot it, then reloaded. I got a sniper rifle and shot it again in the head. The T-rex lunged at me. It killed itself and took off half my health.
'Game completed, you are free to go,' said the voice.
I was ejected out of the PlayStation.

'What a day.' I muttered, 'I'm going back to bed!'

Chris Davies (10)
Barton School

A Day In The Life Of David Beckham

I woke up, got out of bed, went downstairs and there were silk curtains, leather chairs and golden door handles. I walked over to the window and peered through the curtains. I saw cameras, microphones, TV vans and reporters. I told myself, I had a long night last night, I'm just dreaming. Something strange told me I was no longer Mark Day, but David Beckham. I stood there for a few minutes thinking about all the goals David has scored for England and all the cool stuff he must do. I smiled and opened the front door and shouted, 'Good morning, Manchester!'

I had to take Brooklyn for a morning walk, well, that was what Vicky told me anyway.
'Do you want to go to the park?' I asked Brooklyn.
'Yes,' Brooklyn burbled.
So we set off. When we got there, I saw some local kids called Tom, Jim and Dave. 'Look, it's David Beckham!' screeched Jim to Tom and Dave. They ran over to me.
'Can we have your autograph?' asked Tom.
'Yes, of course you can,' I told them.
They asked me to play and I said yes. It was me and Brooklyn versus Tom, Jim and Dave. Well, Brooklyn sort of sat there mumbling on about goodness knows what! The score ended up 4-3 to them, I let them win. Being Beckham, I wasn't exactly going to lose to a bunch of kids if I was trying!

We went home and had supper with my team mates, they were already there when I got home. I got told off by Vicky, she's a bit like my mum really. We talked for ages after we had all finished eating, all thirteen of us.

The night had been long and I got up and looked in the mirror. I ran into my mum's room, 'I'm *me* again!' I shouted at my mum. She didn't know what I was going on about, but I was happy anyway!

Mark Day (11)
Barton School

THE PEBBLE

The pebble caught my eye instantly as I wandered along the beach. I picked it up. It felt strangely warm in my hand. I ran back along the beach to where Alice was making a shelter in some rocks. 'Alice! Alice! Look what I've found!' I shouted.

'Wow!' Alice exclaimed.

It was a perfect sphere. I took out my hanky and started to clean it. It glowed amber. Suddenly, everything went black. No, I could see Alice.

'Rub the pebble again,' Alice told me.

Suddenly, I hit hard ground. A man stood in front of me, I squeezed Alice's hand tightly. 'You have been chosen,' he told us.

'Ch-chosen for wh-what?' I stuttered.

'Chosen to defeat the dragon and replace the stone of Arothos, God of Othea, in its place,' he replied.

'How do I get there?'

'Follow that road,' he replied, mystically pointing.

I followed the road. At last, after an all night trek, I found the cave. What I couldn't believe was that the dragon just squealed and ran away! I put the pebble in a hole in the wall . . .

With a thud, I found myself at home.

'Where have you been?' Mum asked.

'Er . . . nowhere,' I replied.

Elspeth Gibbs (9)
Barton School

THE PEBBLE

The pebble caught my eye instantly as I wandered along the beach. I picked it up, it felt warm in my hand. I held it against my chest and lifted it to my nose, the pebble smelt salty. Carefully, I put it in my basket with the other stones I had found. When I got back home, I took the stone out of the basket and held it in my hand. Suddenly the door opened and in came my mother. 'Where have you been?' she shouted. I decided to tell a lie. 'In my room,' I exclaimed.
I felt a hot feeling in my hand, I screamed and dropped the pebble. I quickly ran up the stairs, straight to my room.

The phone rang, it was Jemma, my best friend. She reminded me about her sleep-over party tomorrow night. I had everything ready, for a present I had got her a book of jewellery. I had also got her a friendship bracelet. I rushed back downstairs and picked up the stone. I realised what it was now, it was a lie stone. If you tell a lie while holding it, it will burn your hand.

The next day, I went to Jemma's party with the stone. My worst enemy, Lucy-Anne, was there. She was really nasty to me. I gave Jemma her present and showed her the stone. When it was bedtime, I couldn't find my stone. Jemma's mum told me to look for it in the morning. When morning came, I searched everywhere for it, but I could not find it. I started to cry.

When my mum came to pick me up, Lucy came up to me, she said she was sorry and gave me the stone. From then on we were friends. I realised that the stone was a waste of my time. That evening, I went to the beach with my boat and sailed out into the middle of the sea and dropped my pebble where no one could find it. Then I sadly dawdled home and as I looked back, I could still see a sparkle in the water.

Sophie Harding (10)
Barton School

A Day In The Life Of A Baby Sparrow

It was a long way back, about a year ago . . .

I awoke and I was trapped inside an egg, it was filled with blood cells and gooey stuff. I wriggled and made the egg crack. I stepped out of the egg and from then on I was a sparrow.
A bird flew over to me and fed me a big, fat, juicy worm. After giving me the worm, she flew off again. Then I heard a noise behind me, I turned around and saw another sparrow.

I stuck my head through a bush and I saw my back garden with a slide, climbing frame and my cat, Tea Bag. Suddenly I fell. Tea Bag ran towards me and pounced. The sparrow that fed me took me back to the nest. It was becoming dark, so I fell asleep.

I woke up in my bedroom with Tea Bag at my feet. I got out of bed and looked in the mirror . . . I was human again.

Laura Packman (10)
Barton School

A Day In the Life Of A Kitten

It was nine o'clock at night. I was so tired, I couldn't keep my eyes open and then fell asleep in my warm, bouncy bed.

I woke up and opened my eyes. I could only see black and white. Then suddenly I felt fur on me and whiskers and a long, skinny tail. I jumped out of my bed. I had shrunk! I had four legs. I opened the door with my head, because it wasn't closed properly. I walked downstairs because I had never walked downstairs with four legs before. I went into the kitchen, my tummy started to rumble. I was really hungry. I looked around the room. I then went into the dining room. I jumped on the table to see if there was any food there, but there wasn't, so I miaowed. I waited, nobody came. I tried to use the cat flap for the first time and I did it. I looked around the garden, I saw a leaf, I started to chase it, until I saw an animal in the air. It landed in the garden.
Is that a flying rabbit, I thought. Oh, it's a bird!
I started chasing that instead of the leaf and . . . and, I caught it! I tried to eat it. I couldn't, so I took it through the cat flap with me. My owner was in the kitchen.
'What is that, Jasmine?' my owner asked.
I miaowed. She took the bird and put it in the bin. There were feathers everywhere. My owner gave me my breakfast. Yes, I thought, at last!

My owner swept all the feathers up and threw the feathers away with the bird. I was looking forward to the bird for my afters.

It was afternoon, I was exhausted. I jumped onto the boiler and jumped into my basket. My owner came along and stroked me and kissed me on my head. I rolled over. My owner tickled my tummy. I loved it and fell asleep.

It was morning. My mum called me for school, I was still in my bed. All my fur and whiskers and my tail had gone. I got out of bed, I felt quite disappointed that I wasn't a kitten anymore.

Catharine McLaughlin (10)
Barton School

THE PEBBLE

The pebble caught my eye instantly as I walked along the beach. I picked it up. It felt strangely warm in my hand. It was glowing. I looked at it wondering what to do with it. After a while, I decided to take it to a science lab. I put it in my pocket and walked to the lab, it was only a short way away.

When I got there, the receptionist remarked, 'This is no place for children!'
'It's OK, Dorien!' Dr Atom told her, 'He's a VIP!'

A few minutes later we were in his office.
'So what brings you here?'
I told him about the pebble glowing and how I had found it. He asked me if he could run some tests on it and I said yes. Just then, he vanished! Ten minutes later, he reappeared. I took it home and put it on my shelf. That night I had a strange dream, it was about me and the place where Dr Atom had disappeared to. It kept playing over and over. The next day, I got up and went in the backyard and buried it, hoping never to see it again.

Chris Hardwick (11)
Barton School

THE PEBBLE

The pebble caught my eye instantly as I wandered along the beach. I picked it up. It felt strangely warm in my hand. I put it in my pocket and I ran home. I put it on my desk and I climbed into bed. The next morning it was the weekend, so I stayed in bed and watched TV. The sun was getting bright, so I got out of bed. I got dressed and played on my computer.

I saw the pebble. It stared at me. I put it back in my pocket and went to the shops. As I went to the counter, someone tried to steal it. I turned around and yelled!

On Monday, I went to work. Some man again tried to steal it, but he did not get it. When I got home, I had tea in front of the TV. The news came on and said, '. . . there are only two of these pebbles in the world. The other one is in the sea.'

I telephoned the queen and she gave me a million pounds!

Josh Wright (10)
Barton School

A Day In The Life Of Britney Spears

I was woken up this morning by a loud knock at my door, *thud, thud!* I dragged myself wearily out of bed and stumbled to my bedroom door. Everyone knew I didn't get in till midnight last night, but this is how my usual day goes . . .

This morning at 9am, I was woken by my annoying bodyguard who brought me an awful, dry celery stick for breakfast, which I was forced to eat because there was a lot to do before a 2pm lunch! I didn't even get to choose that, but sometimes I manage to sneak a nice greasy hamburger. After, I was dragged out of bed to get ready for the first thing on my busy schedule. (Today, Wednesday, is probably the busiest day of the week!) I had to get the recording of my new single! Although that was very tiring, I did get an hour off singing to let my voice rest before having another shot at recording.

Next was probably the most stressing part of my day, interviews with magazines, because they always bring up a question about Justin, or my family. There is always, 'Do you have time for a personal life being a singer?'
In the end, I just say, 'No comment,' (although I want the public to know about me, it is hard to make a decision on my personal life.)

After the few stressing interviews, I was whisked off through the blinding cameras and press to the first shot of my new video, 'Cinderella.' The dance I have to do is quite hard and I have practised lots and lots, but I still don't get all of the moves! When I try to tell my choreographer, she just says I will get it when I do it all the way through, but I won't!

When I eventually got a break, the time 12pm, my feet were killing and I was really hungry, especially when I had another two hours to go before lunch. After my break, I had to run through my dance six more times, then another dance, (which I found really easy) two times, for my concert in two weeks! I mean, two weeks is ages away and I know this one off by heart!

Lunch finally came around two hours later. I managed to grab myself a box of chips, but I had hardly any time before I was spotted by the press in the café! I got dragged back into the dance studio and was told to get straight back to practising. Then I had to go and practise my songs for a stage rehearsal tomorrow, which I knew would take all day! Being a singer isn't just about singing, it is about being you.

Stephanie Freeman (11)
Earith Primary School

A DAY IN THE LIFE OF MY BEST FRIEND'S CAT

I gave a little jump as something warm moved along my back. I opened my eyes quickly to see my owner stroking me. 'You are a fat cat!' she said. I watched as Archie came padding out of the hall looking jealous. He jumped onto the sofa. 'Ow!' screamed my human, 'Don't fight over me!'

Soon, in came the baby. As quick as a wink, I was off the sofa and running down the hallway, but my baby pet was after me! Yes, you've guessed it . . . I was trapped!

Baby pet picked me up and took me into the living room. She loves pulling my tail. I put up with this for five minutes and then I decided to scamper. Down the hall and out the back door. I fell asleep in the sandpit, until I smelt something delicious. I ran into the kitchen where there was an extremely big pet. I started on my dinner, but was picked up by baby pet again. I was then taken into the playroom where I was dressed from head to toe in dolls' clothes! I mean, can you believe it? how stupid do they think I am? Once I was out of those stupid dolls' clothes, I decided I'd had enough for today, so I went back to my nap on the sofa.

Kasia Kaluza-Gilbert (10)
Earith Primary School

THE WOLVES STRIKE BACK

Steven sat down, panting. Ever since he and his brothers had stopped the wolves from getting the magical orb of power, newspaper reporters and crazy interviewers had chased them around. Now, since the door was locked, they were trying to bungee jump in through the chimney. Steven looked out of the window, sighed and looked away again. Steven didn't know exactly what had made him look up again, but he did know that it had been brown and extremely hairy. Steven gasped as his mind landed on what the creature had resembled. 'No,' he stuttered, 'it can't be true!'

Steven consulted his brothers, Andrew and James, who suggested that he looked at the Legendary Journal. When they had removed it from the silver capsule, they unrolled it and looked all over it, but they found nothing that would help them until Andrew decided to look on the back. There, they found out that there was an orb that could heal any living thing. The only theory that entered their heads was that the wolves had obtained the healing orb and used it. 'Tomorrow, we will try and locate them and steal the orb,' confirmed Andrew, who then started a 'we will need' list. This is what it said so far:

3 swords,
3 health packs,
1 Jeep,
1 rope.

All three of them went to bed that night knowing that the wolves would be hard to beat, but not one of them suspected that in two hours time they would lose one of the members of their group. Two hours later, something was creaking. It was the wolves opening the bedroom door. You know that, and I know that, but the three pigs did not. One of the wolves picked up Andrew and put him in a sack. When the two pigs woke up, they found their brother gone, maybe never to return . . .

Max Hutchins (9)
Earith Primary School

12TH JULY SHE ROSE AGAIN

On the 12th two hundred years ago, do you know what happened? Let me tell you . . .

There was a young girl, Orlanda, around twenty-one, and she was a great leader of an ancient army. She was a princess and she loved her people dearly. The sun beat down on the sand as the ancient protectors lay low and a sand mummy began to twirl. The sand rose rapidly and Orlanda fell to the ground, her dress weighing her down. She was stuck and she knew it!

Orlanda managed to escape the rising sand. No one knows how, but she did and she ruled another year. But then . . .

'She has to die, she's evil.' The army began to protest that they needed a new leader. Orlanda loved her people so much that when she heard this, she was sacrificed at the young age of twenty-two. Our village tells this story, so tonight I'm going with my family to visit her body.

Later that night the museum had just opened, so we went inside. Her body lay there, cold and still, with a gold plate in her hands.

Later, once my family had gone to the next room, I took the plate! *Smash!* It hit the side and scattered into three pieces. Still holding one piece in my hand, I saw the markings engraved in the gold plate. It was the seal! I'd broken the seal, the mummy will rise again! By the time I'd pulled myself together and put the broken seal back, my family were calling me.

I got ready for bed and climbed under the duvet, but the smash echoed in my head. I heard it! A slight, muffled plod along the landing coming towards my door. I lay doing nothing, I couldn't move out of fright. It had frozen my body. It came closer to my door. My mum flung open the door and started yelling at me. I was unsure why. She looked full of rage. She held three pieces of broken plate in her hands, with her feet tapping on the floorboards. I knew I was for it!

Emma Sewell (10)
Earith Primary School

GHOST STORY

A few days ago, I was going to a Hallowe'en party at my mum's friend's house. I was happy and excited. I decided to wear my witch costume, which was a big, black cloak, a pointed hat and I attached a big, green, ugly nose to make me look scary.

On the day of the party I got ready and called on my friend, Steven, who was dressed as a monster wearing a huge face mask and large, fat fingers. He looked ugly and frightening. We took loads of sweets, like chewy sweets and gob stoppers to give to trick-or-treaters. We gave half a dozen sweets away to trick-or-treaters and then went trick-or-treating. I took my super soaker and said to Steven, 'If they don't give sweets, we will soak them.'

We knocked on the door and shouted, 'Trick or treat!' My mum's friend Trudy gave us some red-hot sweets and we went in. We went to the cupboard and hung our big, scary cloaks up and then it was time to have dinner.
We had dinner and had to beg them to go Hallowe'ening, but they said, 'Let your dinner go down.' So we did, and we went by ourselves.

We knocked on the door at one house, they wouldn't give us any sweets, so we soaked them and ran in the park to hide. We heard this weird noise and what seemed like a ghost was coming out of its grave. It was my gran's grave. We went over to it and it looked nothing like her, so we started running. The ghost started following us. We were horrified and ran and Steven fell in a manhole. I tried to get him out and fell in myself. The ghost came and helped me up. I woke up in hospital a few days later, with Steven, and we never went trick-or-treating again for quite a few years . . .

Aaron Andrus (11)
Earith Primary School

A Day In The Life Of The Queen

It was my Golden Jubilee today. I was so excited, but nervous. We visited schools and then after that, we went to my party. When I say 'we', I mean my children and me. We went to a few schools. My personal favourite was Earith School.

We went there last, but there was a certain buzz to it. All the children were standing round the gate. We drove in with my corgis barking like mad. As soon as we got to the parking lot, they must have run as quick as they could because they were all surrounding me, but there was a certain little person with ginger hair. She was quite short and she was wearing pigtails, but when I started to walk out of the parking lot, she was gone. I never actually found out her name, because whenever I tried to find her, she was never there.

We attended the buffet in the school field, all the children looked like they were having a superb time. I was never left alone, a large crowd of children was always following me. After a wonderful tea, which we had on the field, we went to all the classes. The last class we went to was year 5/6 and then I looked around to see if I could spot the small girl, but I never found her.

And what a surprise! Sir Elton John was there. He was holding a microphone on the stage and started to sing the national anthem as a rap. I mean, what terrible taste! I could stand it no longer and had to put my hands over my ears. How dare they ruin *my anthem!*

Ten minutes later, I went back to the car park. I said goodbye and got in the car. I was still in shock to think that Sir Elton would do such a thing. I think today was one of the strangest days of my life. How could someone sing *my* anthem as a *rap.* I am so *cross!*

Nicole McGarrey (9)
Earith Primary School

A Day In The Life Of Victoria Beckham

It was coming to the end of the day when the football players came over and had a drink to enjoy before the game tomorrow. I got out a board game called UNO and it was a laugh. I played it with David. We had another drink when it was coming up to nine o'clock.

At nine o'clock, most people had gone, but some were left in my house. We had hardly any drinks left in the cupboard! We had to walk up to the shop to get some more. When everyone went home, David and I tidied up the living room and the kitchen.

We then watched TV and had another drink before we went to bed. We were so tired, we crashed out on the sofa until a big cry came from upstairs. It was certainly David's turn this time to go and see to the baby!

Hannah Wilson (11)
Earith Primary School

A DAY IN THE LIFE OF MY CAT, FOREST

Humans! They think they can control us, but they can't!

I slept on the girl's bed last night. It was so annoying. 'Zzzz, wriggle, zzzz, wriggle,' she kept me awake all night. I decided two can play at that game. 'Miaow, miaow!' Next was scratch power. I sat for ages scratching at the door, when finally the monster awoke. Rubbing her eyes, the zombie-like creature reached for the door slowly. It opened! I was out of there as quick as a blink.

I walked around for a little while. Where to go next? Aha! The woman's room. The door was open a touch. I made the biggest entrance ever! I slammed the door open and let out the biggest cry in history. It worked! She arose and patted the bed next to her. I couldn't resist the perfect companion for the rest of the night. As morning arose, I stretched out across the bed. A large hand started coming closer. It rubbed my belly to my heart's content. I rolled over and purred so I stayed there for the last few minutes of the night. The woman got out of bed, I followed. Down the stairs, along the hall and she opened the door. There in front of me was the biggest butterfly ever! My bum wiggled. My eyes stared, I pounced! I caught it in one paw. I was so pleased with myself! But that was short-lived - it flew away. It was one big game of chase! After a night of hardly any sleep, I sat in the sunniest part of the garden. I had a long wash. Mum soon appeared, so I quickly lay down and went to sleep in the sun!

Bethan Pritchard (10)
Earith Primary School

THE HENDERSONS

Suddenly the sky grew dark, the moon was not in sight. The Henderson boys just ignored it. They kept the people of Brighton scared, even if they didn't like it.

Soon the people of Brighton found it hard to become scared and the Henderson boys became bored, so they went to the joke shop to get a couple more jokes. They had loads of fun with their new jokes and soon the people of Brighton once again became annoyed with the Henderson boys and they had a plan.

That night, they blew up some balloons and put white sheets over them, then they let the float past the Henderson boys' bedroom window. As they floated past their window, the Henderson boys thought it was ghosts, so they ran all over Brighton screaming that they'd seen ghosts floating past their window. They all laughed and never had any trouble from the Henderson boys again.

Shaun Smith (11)
Earith Primary School

A DAY IN THE LIFE OF MY CAT CHARLIE

Dear diary,

I woke up this morning on a soft bed that belonged to one of my humans. She seemed to be using, some sort of strange code language 'Zzzz, zzzz, zzzzzzzz . . .' She went on using this language that seemed extremely hard to understand and it got more annoying by the minute. I'd had enough! I decided to wake her up, but couldn't find her face because she had buried it under the large blanket-like thing. I scrambled under and rubbed my wet and soggy nose all over her cheeks and mouth. (I know she hates that, and it always works!) Her language ended, at last peace and quiet, but not for long. Out from my human came a sleepy noise, 'Go away Charlie, I need my sleep.'

My plan wasn't working, so do you know what I did? I annoyed her even more, and more, but eventually she couldn't put up with it any longer! She got up out of bed and stumbled to the kitchen. I was so glad I had woken her up, because she was about to make me my first meal of the day, breakfast! The other cats came and crowded around the giant cupboard full of our meals to come. Ah! The smell of food!

After the hassle of breakfast was over, I decided to go and chase butterflies in the garden with my sister. Phew! It was really wearing me out. After running around, I found a fantastic sunny spot and had a wonderful long sleep.

Miaow!

Daryl Smith (10)
Earith Primary School

THE BLOOD-SUCKING GHOST

I had just come back from school and I had a peculiar feeling that someone was following me. I turned around and saw nothing! I felt a little tap on my shoulder. I turned around and saw a blur of blue light in front of me. I carried on walking; at last I got home and Mum shouted, 'Dinner's ready, Simon.'
I ran into the dining room to get my dinner, 'What is that?' I shouted. 'Your dinner.'
I was staring at a plate of carrots, raw carrots. I ran out of the room and up to my bedroom to play on my game console. I had that funny feeling that someone was there, I turned around and I couldn't believe my eyes, it was a ghost! I was scared stiff. I couldn't move.

I shouted to my mum. She came running up the stairs and the first thing she did was faint.
'More blood for a bloodthirsty ghost,' it said. The ghostly hiss, 'At last, I will be able to drink the blood of a human and become mortal.'
The ghost charged through me and made me faint, it started to suck the blood out of my body. Luckily, my mum awoke and got the vacuum cleaner and sucked the ghost up. My mum raced me to the hospital. They gave me a lot, and I mean a lot, of blood. They told me that I was one of the luckiest boys alive.

Once I got home, my mum asked if I was alright. I felt a bit weary.
'You have just had two gallons of blood pumped into you, you would feel a bit weary!' she said.

Andrew Watson (10)
Earith Primary School

A DAY IN THE LIFE OF SIR ELTON JOHN

I woke up early to 'Candle in the Wind' in my new CD alarm clock. I have always loved that song since I recorded it. Downstairs, the mail had arrived. There weren't very many parcels today, just seventeen. I had a quick breakfast of eggs (two of course), bacon, sausages, toast, black pudding, eggy bread, French toast and wine before getting into my limo to go to the recording studios.

Today I was recording a new song for the Queen's Golden Jubilee party. It's called the modern anthem, which is the national anthem as a rap. I'm not too sure I'll like it. I don't like raps much, but I'll give it a go. All Sirs should be able to do anything, that is one of their skills and singing is definitely one of mine.

After a short lunch break (well, two hours!) I was back at the recording studios being told that I was going to make a video for this stupid song. They wanted me kitted out in a biker jacket and a pair of leather trousers (which are not very nice because they make me look fourteen again. But that isn't that bad, is it?) I agreed, and I don't know why. Probably because I was desperate to get back home.

When I finally did get home (which was in quite a few hours) I found the Queen and her corgis sitting on my couch, the Queen was also drinking a glass of wine! The cheek of her! That wine was for tomorrow's breakfast. I found myself taking her out for dinner and discussing her jubilee celebrations. She kept going on and on about her primary school tour. *Snore!*

Then all I could do was crash onto my deluxe sized bed and sleep. See you about noon tomorrow!

Emma-Louise Hetherington (11)
Earith Primary School

WHO'S THERE?

It was another boring day in Earith. I was on my way home. I walked into the living room and my mum was sitting in a dark corner. 'What is the matter?' I whispered.
'It's your brothers and Lewis.'
'What about them?'
'They have been transported to another world.'
'No!'
I bent down on my hands and knees. Then I stormed into the computer room, then I was transported to the same place. I found Lewis sitting on the floor with a sniper rifle, machine-gun and a shotgun. I picked a rocket launcher and ten C4 Exploris machine-guns and a flame-thrower.

There was a guard at the door and it was all up to me to get us out of here. I woke Lewis up, we got a rock and threw it at the guard who fell straight to the floor.
'Quick, get the keys and let's get out of here.'
Within moments, David and Lewis were down on the monitor when there was a problem. 'There is a *dragon!*' Lewis shouted as loud as he could.
'*Shut up, Lewis!*'
There were some funny things going on down there, like a funny magic going on.

Suddenly the dragons fell to the ground, so we could get past them *alive!* There was a castle in front of us, but guns were everywhere. We grabbed all the C4 Exploris and ran for the castle to destroy it. He ran as fast as he could back and *bang!* The castle was gone and Lewis had saved the day. A genie appeared and all of a sudden, we were back home.

David Newman (11)
Earith Primary School

TABBY, KELLY AND I

It all started on Sunday evening when Tabby first found the strange key. Tabby was a tortoiseshell cat with an extremely inquisitive nature. She came in at the cat flap with the pale metal contraption dangling from her jaws. At first we thought it was a bird. We rushed to take it off her, but then we saw that it was just metal, and too big for her to swallow, so we left it with her.

Slowly the evening passed and night came, leaving us in peace. Morning came and shook our drowsy heads till we woke. Stumbling down the stairs, we headed for breakfast and our mother's call.
'What *have* you given Tabby?' Our mum definitely sounded angry. 'I thought you two knew better.' She scolded and tutted all through breakfast, so Kelly and me ate in silence. When we had finished, we walked slowly upstairs. We changed and came back down to play with Tabby.

I took the metal thing from her and it was then that I noticed the strange inscriptions at each swirly part.
Kelly turned to me, still stroking Tabby. 'I think that's a key. See those swirly bits, they go in the keyhole. And it takes you to a place, the one it says,' she said, pointing to the inscriptions.
I looked at her. She had always had a vast imagination, but she was serious this time. *Really* serious.

'I can think of two reasons for you to be lying. One: you always run away with your tongue. Two: where's the keyhole?' my voice was sharp and annoyed.
Kelly turned towards me with an angry face. 'You're always so mean, discarding my ideas like that. What if I was right? And as for sorry, you don't mean it. We both know it. You're just being all airy-fairy as always.'
'Really, I am sorry. Truly sorry,' I said.
'I'm sorry too, I didn't mean it,' Kelly said.

I picked up the metal thing once more. Turning it over in my hands, I ran my finger over the inscriptions, trying to work out what they meant. What *did* they mean? We accepted the idea that it was a key, or rather I accepted. Eventually, we decided that the only way to make some use of it was to find a lock that it fitted in. Unusually, that didn't take very long. After a week had passed, we found the key fitted into the old-fashioned lock in Kelly's window that we had long since lost the real key to.

The first thing we did was look through the window. We saw an old-fashioned garden bench with tea ready laid out on it. There was a large pond with tall pond weeds growing around the edge of it. A low croaking chorus accompanied all of this. Undoubtedly, toads and frogs made this!

It turned out the key was just a random piece of metal. Our mum had laid out a special lunch for us and our imaginations had taken over.

Helen Mallett (10)
Earith Primary School

THE GUARDIAN: A GHOST STORY

The cobwebs swept across my face. The hairs on my neck stuck up like needles and the dark mansion appeared in front of my eyes. The new place seemed thrilling, yet I felt the screams of the children. I left the maid to clean rooms and to check for any signs of Nazis, as the war was still in progress.

I soon let the children come into the house. They had only taken one step into the house, when they ran out after hearing the housemaid scream. I ran up the stairs in horror, only to find the housemaid lying in a heap, with a slight puddle of blood on the floor!

My lips trembled with fright. Someone, or something, was in the house with them.
'M'am, I'm sorry to have startled you like that, but someone was calling me into the room. I thought it was you at first, but then something began to pull at my leg. I almost died of fright myself.'

The door downstairs slammed shut as the children gradually walked into the room. I began to help the maid up and took her down into the kitchen to clean up the cut on her leg. I showed the children to their rooms. The door slammed shut and I heard the turning of a key.

I knew someone was in the house with them . . .

I looked under the crack of the door to see where the person should have been, but all I saw was a clear space. Screams soon filled my head. After one hour, the house was somehow rejecting me. Luckily for us, we were locked in the only room with an open window. The other windows were rusted shut.

The following evening, strange faces began to appear on the floor and windows. I kept trying to clean them off, but they kept reappearing. I heard screams from the living room where I had left the children to do their homework. I ran into the room with my heart pounding, thinking that ghosts were attempting to kill the children. I went into the hall to see the children and the maid floating in the air.

'I'm sorry to say this, M'am, but I'm a ghost. I died in eighteen eighty-one. Quite depressing really. I was killed during the stakeout that the family were doing,' blurted the maid in a guilty, but proud tone.

'But how can I see you?' I asked, questioning the maid.

'You're a ghost too,' replied the maid.

The room filled with colours and three people stood in the middle of the room. They were chanting, when one yelled, 'We have been accompanied by two, no three ghosts.'

'See, these are the true guardians of the house. They bought it seven years ago,' exclaimed the maid.

I slowly walked away in shame. My life was now officially over.

Daniel Bainbridge (11)
Earith Primary School

A NIGHT IN THE LIFE OF HEDGE, A HEDGEHOG

11.03.02. 12:00 in the morning.

Dear diary,

Something terrible has just happened. I'm sure you remember Great Aunt Jibbett, well (sob) this morning as she was taking her exercise. She had just about crossed the road, so far it was the fastest time ever, but it wasn't fast enough! The purplish-blue Ford Mondeo was much faster!

I'll write a bit later, be careful . . .

11.03.02. 9:00 in the evening.

Because of the recent tragedy, Mum has forbidden us from going out of the borough, (which is unfair) because now I can't choose my own slugs and I like the long ones with the crunchy, spiral tops. Dad always hunts for the small plain ones (ugh!) I wouldn't complain if it weren't important, which it is. I might never have seen Spiky again, and that's serious. I'd have become bored, lonely and I wouldn't know the news of the outside world. I need a plan . . . and fast!

But I have just that . . .

12.05.02. 4:00 in the morning.

Today I have done some hard work, in secrecy all day. Well, most of the day. The first thing I did was sneak out of the borough which, might I add, was immensely difficult. I had to dig a hole in the side of my bedroom, and then I had trouble navigating because of the light. I was blinded for half an hour.

Soon Mum would know that somehow, I'd gotten out of the borough (then I'd be in trouble) but I had to carry on, so I just pretended it was dark, which helped, but the obvious daytime didn't.

Soon I got to my location - the Jones's garage, which was a very dangerous place, but for my job it was perfect, except for the heights. On the table three feet above me was just the thing I needed, but to get to it, I'd need to climb a slippery steel table leg, which Is not easy, let me tell you. No offence, diary, but I bet you've never done anything nearly as difficult.

But let's go back to the garage. I found a structure made out of metal sticks. Humans obviously used it to climb on, so I tried it. I put out my front paws, grabbed the next twig, pulled myself up and repeated this until I got in line with the table. It was a good thing the climbing structure was so near the table, or the leap I made would have been in vain. But I'm glad to say I made it safely. Now, where was it?

After what seemed like hours, I finally found it. *Tacks*, it said. Perfect. I pushed it off. It didn't spill as it was sealed. I pushed off a rather large sponge (weird to have in a garage, but it's their choice), I jumped onto it (rather cleverly I think.) I pushed it into the middle of the road and then I opened it with my small claws. I tipped it with my snout. All over the road they poured. Then I went home.

Mum, thanks to my little brother, was not mad. When I got home and filled in the hole, I found out that my brother had told Mum I had locked the door and gone to sleep. As she always wanted me to go to sleep, she went off and never suspected he was lying.

12.05.02. 10:00 in the evening.

My plan worked. The road was condemned, nine out of ten cars got flat tyres on the road. Now I can go out all I like, as no cars come near us.

Hedge H.

Dylan Dearnaley (10)
Earith Primary School

A DAY IN THE LIFE OF MICHAEL OWEN

I stepped out of the coach with the England squad by my side. I entered the stadium with great relief, for I had just travelled for six hours. Once the squad and I were finished changing, we returned to the green turf, which we had lost on against Argentina in 1998. We spread out into our positions, ready to thrash the opposite team.

I stood still with the tension still growing in my body. A few minutes later, Argentina entered the pitch and the crowd started roaring in great excitement and started to sing the Argentinean national anthem repeatedly. The referee quickly blew his whistle, the crowd stopped singing and the game was under way. Beckham passed it to me, I passed it up the wing to Heskey, I ran in the box, the ball came high, I headed it and boom! The ball was in the back of the net. 1-0!

Twenty minutes later, the ball was on the penalty spot in our area! David Seaman eyed the ball as it came surging towards him. He opened his hands and leaped for dear life, the ball smacked against his hands, but luckily he got a firm grip on the ball, saving it from flying into the back of the net. The squad and I screamed in happiness, in line with the crowd, for we could have just been saved from getting knocked out. The referee blew his whistle again and I walked off with my heart pounding.

Later on, I was getting a drink when Nicky Butt came walking up to me and started blabbing about if I don't start playing better, I will be subbed with him. But I just ignored him!

The second half had started. For about forty minutes nothing really happened until Batistuta pulled back a goal in the dying minutes, but we were sure to score another. But we didn't, it went into penalties and it was all up to me to score. The keeper stared at me and surprisingly, not the ball. I took five steps back and then quickly ran forward, I pelted the ball to find it going straight past the post. The crowd froze and so did I, until I heard a voice behind me. 'Run, Michael, run!' it shouted, so I did, but as soon as I got an inch away from the ball, the keeper jumped out for it and grabbed it from under my feet.

I looked around me, totally embarrassed. I dropped to the floor to the sight of all the Argentineans dancing around me. We had lost again . . .

Johnathan Griffiths (10)
Earith Primary School

JUST ANOTHER WALK

One day, as normal, I took the dog for a walk. I saw a bunny. Thinking it was a normal one, I picked it up. It had some sort of collar on it. I showed Mum, but she said, 'Put it down.'
I groaned back, 'OK.'
(Mum thought I had put it back, but I didn't.) However, I put a stone down and I sneaked it home. I went straight to my room and took off the collar: it was some sort of magic collar.

As soon as I took it off, I was in a different world. It was really weird. First I picked some flowers for my mum, but as soon as I picked them, they melted straight away! I was amazed! (I licked it to see what it was: it was chocolate).

I went to a river nearby - it was blueberry milkshake. I caught a strawberry jellyfish, it was tasty, very tasty indeed. I looked up and saw a lollipop lady. I said, 'Could you help me please?'
'Sure, come with me, this is the wonder world.'

It was really fantastic and looked really tasty. People rode about in liquorice cars. The houses were made of chocolate sponge fingers. It was unbelievable! It was any child's dream come true.

In the distance, I saw a bright light. I heard my mum calling me. I didn't know where I was until I saw the drill coming towards my mouth. Then I could see that the bunny laying on the dentist's chair . . .

Karleen Briggs (10)
Stanground St John's School

THE WALLS OF BLOOD

Chapter 1. Let's Go On Holiday!

I want to go to Ibiza. I want to go to America. No! we are gong to Winsonbirg. So we got packed and went there. My name's Chriswiz and I have an older brother named Joejoe.

When we got there, it wasn't so bad. There was a big shopping centre, a massive castle and not too many houses. First we went to the house. Mum said that we should get unpacked, but I can't believe how long we are staying in this place. I mean, two weeks is enough.

Chapter 2. What Is In There?

After we all went shopping, Dad went home and the rest of us went to the abandoned castle. We walked up the pathway, I got my gun ready, the door opened . . .

Chapter 3. The Castle.

We went in. The walls were covered with fresh blood. A zombie had been killed and the blood had splattered everywhere. There was a chair in the room and there was a letter which described a centaur. At night it changes into objects. Watch out because the last person who saw it sat in a chair which turned into a centaur. We ran through the door, it chased us. I pulled out my gun and shot it. The centaur died, blood was flying all over us, but we carried on running. We were free!

Christopher Morton (10)
Stanground St John's School

A Day In The Life Of Shakira
(Up to the concert)

06:00. Gotta get up and get ready for my concert in seven hours. Why do lush pop stars have to get up so early? I want to stay in bed till ten. Oh well, I'm not gonna get up while I'm hanging around in bed am I?

06:30. Just got out of the shower. I feel a lot more awake now. What am I going to wear? My pink hipsters and my blue boob tube, or my pink hipsters and my purple, one-sleeved top? Decisions, decisions.

07:09. Just boarding my stretched limo. Goodness, I'm tired, but I've got to get to the studio to record my new song, *Whenever, Whenever.* I'd better rehearse it in Spanish . . .

09:38. Done the album. Sheesh, AJ is grumpy this morning. Did he get up on the wrong side of the bed or something?

11:56. Nearly two hours till the concert begins. I'm really nervous. It's my first concert ever, but it happens to all pop stars, right?

12:56. Just getting my mic on. Then I am gonna run on the stage like I've never run in my whole life!

15:58. Great!

Hayley Boyden (9)
Stanground St John's School

SPOOKY STORY

One misty and cold night near an old haunted house, near a dark and droopy river, there were four boys playing in the park, when there was a horrible noise. The boys were saying to one and other, 'What is it? Will it get us?'
Then the oldest one said, 'It's only the wind blowing, don't be scared.'

The next day after school, the boys went down to the park and they stayed there until it started to get a little dark, then the youngest boy said, 'I'm going home because I don't want to hear the noise again.;
Then the other boys shouted, 'Chicken, chicken!'
All of a sudden there was a loud scream and it was coming from the old haunted house. The boys ran to the nearest house.
'M . . . Mu . . . Mum, there's a screaming coming from that old haunted house.'
'Is there?'
'Yes, we all heard it.'
'OK, I will go and see, but if there's not, then you are all in trouble and I will tell all of your mums.'

Tom, Paul, Tony, Dan and Tom's mum went to see what was happening and to Tom's mum's surprise, she heard screaming. Tom's mum had her mobile on her, so she got her mobile out and called the police. When she got off the phone, there was no more screaming and when the police arrived, they went in the old haunted house, then they came back out . . . so what had they really heard?

Holli Mayo (10)
Stanground St John's School

A Day In The Life Of A Brachiosaurus

One morning I was walking through the forest looking for my breakfast, wet, soggy leaves. Yum! Yum! You must know that it was raining yesterday. Don't be scared, I am a vegetarian dinosaur and I only eat plants. I am the first dinosaur to plod the Earth.

I eventually found my favourite tree that had plenty of leaves. Once I had finished eating them, I went to my favourite waterhole. I was that thirsty I drank it all up! When I was walking, I felt like I was a walking swimming pool, so I went for a rest.

One hour later, I went for a nice plod, then I heard a roaring sound so I went to check it out. It took me four minutes with my long, strong legs to get there. Unfortunately, it was a T-rex, so I said, 'Oi you, shut up! You are going to wake the world!' I knew it would be safe because his round belly showed he had just eaten.

'Shut up yourself, mate, or I will make you lunch,' said the T-rex.

I said, 'What is the matter?'

'I have a toothache,' said the T-rex.

'I can sort it out if you like. I will just pull it out, OK?' I stated.

'OK,' said the T-rex, nervously.

'Ready. 1, 2, 3, pull! There we go, it is out.'

'Thanks mate, you are a pal. See you tomorrow,' he said.

That is how I made friends with a meat-eating dinosaur.

James Liddell (8)
Welland Primary School

A Day In The Life Of A Penguin

One cold day in the Antarctic, I was outside playing with my friends, so I asked them if they wanted to go for a swim in the sea. Then after a while, I jumped out and landed on my feet, but I tripped over. I got up and walked away. As I was walking, I met up with my girlfriend, so we went swimming again to get some dinner.

We swam underwater and I love it underwater, because in the water I can glide around like a submarine. I'm so clumsy on land because of my large, webbed feet that I prefer to be rocketing around in the ocean. We swam and we swam until we caught some fish. It didn't take us very long to catch our favourite fishy treats.

The fish tasted so lovely I forgot where I was and the ocean is a dangerous place if you go out too far. All of a sudden, I opened my eyes and to my surprise, I noticed a shark, so I swam for my life. I eventually reached the shore and I was puffing and panting badly. That is the last time I go too far out in the ocean!

Daniel Martin (9)
Welland Primary School

A Day In The Life Of A Tree

I've lived in the forest for two hundred years. I'm really proud of my trunk, it's the widest I've ever had in two hundred years. I've grown many different shapes and sizes.

'I need some water up here, root!' I said.

I have a tree called Willow next to me.

'Who are you talking to?' Willow asked.

'Myself, is that alright with you?'

'Yes, it's alright!' he replied.

'You're just jealous because I have a bird's nest on my beautiful branches and you haven't!'

The birds had spent all summer collecting twigs and feathers to build their nest. Eventually I saw, when the mother got up, that there were three eggs in the nest that she was keeping warm. The other day she said to me, 'You're going to be an auntie!' I was so excited, I just couldn't wait.

At that moment, I saw a hole in one of the eggs. I was so delighted, I waved my branches and one of the birds flew away. I thought it was frightened because I had waved my branches around, but when it came back, it had some worms in its mouth. A little head popped out of the egg and I realised it was a little chick. I said to myself, 'I'm going to be the best tree auntie ever!'

Katie Thorogood (8)
Welland Primary School

A Day In The Life Of A Barn Owl

I live in an old hay barn with my husband. He swoops slowly across the trees and hedges, across the rolling countryside, hunting for small brown mice for us to eat. I've just laid a clutch of five smooth, white eggs, which will grow into little barn owls. I have to sit on them to keep the eggs warm. I gobbled up a small brown mouse which my husband had brought to me. Presently, the eggs hatched.

The chicks are growing bigger and bigger every day. They're getting too big for the nest, so we went for a fly with the chicks. We flew to visit my family. They're impressive flyers and it was good that they made it to the family's barn. The chicks have powerful wings and wise eyes. They must take after me.

It comes to the time when the chicks are ready to hunt for themselves. I'm gliding around to try and spy a rodent while my children are watching eagerly. That one looks delicious to eat. I'll teach my babies to do it just like me. They will be the best owl hunters in the world.

Adam Jackson (9)
Welland Primary School

A Day In The Life Of A Dolphin

I love the feel of the water tickling my spine. Even more, I love playing with my friends. I hate to be on my own. Dolphins are very sociable animals you know. Another thing I love about the wide ocean is that I can pop up to the top of the ocean to breathe and to have a look at what's going on.

One day when I was being my usual nosy self, I spotted something strange moving in the water. My curiosity made me glide through the water and get a closer look. This is what I saw, it was a beautiful mermaid with lovely blonde hair which was like gold and she had all different coloured scales down her tail. She was gorgeous. She was swimming and gliding through the water. The mermaid was getting closer and closer to me. She came up to me and offered me some seaweed.

I said, 'No thank you.'

The mermaid spun me round on my fins, but then she glided back through the water and was nowhere in sight. I swam after her like a rocket until I caught up with her.

I said, 'Don't go away, please play with me.'

The mermaid nodded her head, I thought she was saying OK, so I suggest a game of hide-and-seek. First of all she counted and went to hide. We played hide-and-seek until sunset. I had made the best friend ever!

Leoni Moseley (9)
Welland Primary School

A Day In The Life Of A Volcano

I'm the fiercest mountain in the world and I can take up lots of land. Everybody's scared of me. People die because of my lava - it covers the countryside. I love to see my lava coming down my sides. I like to ride down massive hills and play with other lava, although I wish I could walk like other people.

One day, I was standing there bored, when a man came along in a funny silver thing and stared at me, so I erupted. The funny silver thing that I assume was a human, made strange noises and made me even angrier, so I let out even more lava. The man ran away as fast as he could, luckily my lava was slow, so the man got away.

After the eruption, there was wood and fire everywhere. I'd used up all my lava so I was sad. No more lava to come out of me anymore, I was extinct.

Thomas McGlynn (9)
Welland Primary School

A Day In The Life Of A Penguin

Sometimes I look at myself and think what a beautiful bird I am. I've got large, webbed feet and a wonderful round belly and short, stubby legs. I suppose the only thing wrong with me is that I keep falling over, but I can't help it, my feet are too big. I may be clumsy on land, but I'm a great swimmer and when I want to come out of the water, I just have to get out by climbing on the ice.

When I'm in the water, all I'm doing is zooming around catching fish and squid like a rocket. I don't get cold though, because my blubber keeps me warm. It's beautiful gliding through the majestic sea, but sometimes I feel scared because of the eels, they like eating penguins. Oh well, I'd better go and catch my food now.

I rather like it in the sea, there's a nice view. I can see all the plants and different fish. I also love being on the ice when the sun is gleaming. In all, I love being a penguin.

Carl Pate (9)
Welland Primary School

A Day In The Life Of A Hamburger

It's cold in this freezer. I've been in this freezer since I was put in this packet with my quarter-pounder friends: James, Adam and Carl. We can't wait to get out of this freezer. Every morning we hear the door open and we pray it's us. After two days of dreaming, it was our turn.

It is certainly warmer being cooked, in fact, I'm beginning to get rather hot. I guess we're being cooked.
'Yes, we are!' exclaimed James.
Seconds later, I heard Adam say, 'Thank goodness we are in these jackets.'
'Are we in bed?' I asked.
'I'm not sure,' Carl replied.
'No, we are in a bag.'
'Hey, we're moving!'
'What's that noise?'
'It's a car!'

Two minutes later, I was face to face with an ugly human. I thought he was the ugliest thing I had ever seen, but he ate me in one bite. He then followed me with a milkshake. I lay there in his stomach for a while, wishing I was back in the freezer, and then I was digested and I disappeared.

Alex Bedford (9)
Welland Primary School

A Day In The Life Of My Puppy, Ruby

My puppy, Ruby, wakes up at about 8:00am from her peaceful sleep. She stretches her long brown legs and has a huge yawn. She has her breakfast, then she sneaks ever so quietly upstairs and explores. When she gets tired of that, she plays with her small yellow rugby ball. Now, it's getting to the stage where she's falling asleep. She wakes up after a relaxing hour and decides to go outside. Unfortunately, she meets a tubby black and white cat. Now instead of leaving it alone, she decides to have a staring competition with it. The cat doesn't like it, the cat starts to miaow at Ruby and Ruby barks, really loud. Now it's starting to get out of hand, such as scratching and barking. Finally, after about twenty seconds the cat runs away. That proves that the cat was scared. Now she just lounges around the house looking for a nice spot to relax in. She wakes up because of the fine, pleasant smell of her tea. After she's had her tea, she goes on an hour's walk. When she gets back, she goes to bed and dreams of sweet and delightful adventures.

Jodie McLaren (10)
Westfield Junior School

VIRUS WATCH

One day, two men go to Argos to get a Virus Watch to see what it is like. They buy the black watch and head home to play. They play on it for a long time, but it opens up and sucks them in.
'You are in the watch and you have to collect Virus Fifty.'

Ben Marshall went with Jack Chaffe to get Virus Fifty. It was across the roads. Ben went for the challenge, he had five lives and he had four roads to cross. He made it with one life spare. He got it.

Next, they had to get Virus Seventy-Nine. Jack Chaffe was attacked with bombs and guns, but he managed to get the virus. They had to battle to get the last virus, Virus Thirty, with one life left each. They fought really hard and they both won.

Bang! They appeared back at home.

Jack Marshall (9)
Westfield Junior School

HARRY POTTER AND THE GHOST STORY

One day, Harry Potter was asleep under the stairs. When he got up, he looked at his scar, his scar was red, which Voldermort had gave him. It had gotten worse every time he looked at it. The Dursleys were eating their breakfast when Mr Dursley said, 'Where's Potter?'
'I'll go and get him,' said Mrs Dursley.

Harry Potter was brushing his brown hair. When he got out of the cupboard, he saw a letter saying his name and Hogwarts. Harry was very happy, he looked forward to it. Just then, everything started to shake, lots of letters came from Hogwarts, Mr Dursley was shouting and screaming and then he said, 'We're going to a different country, far away from here.'

After about an hour, a man knocked on the door, he was huge. He said to Harry, 'Come on, we're getting out of here.'

The next day they were off. When Harry was on the Hogwarts Express, a boy with red hair called Ron said to Harry, 'Can I sit with you? Everywhere else is full.'
Harry said, 'Yes.'
Two minutes later, a woman came with a trolley and she said, 'Anything you want, boys?'
Ron said, 'No, I've got something.'
Harry said, 'Well, I'll buy the lot.'
When they got there, they saw Hermione.
Ron said, 'She's pretty.'
Harry said, 'Come on, let's move on!'
A ghost got Harry Potter and threw him in the river. Harry got murdered, everyone was sad. The ghost was Lord Voldermort. Voldermort ran away and that was the end of Harry Potter.

Usman Ali (10)
Westfield Junior School

A GHOST STORY

Once upon a time, in a town called St Ives, there were two boys called Ben Chaffe and Jack Smith-Chambers, who were best friends. At school one day, they met up with an enemy called Ryan and his best friend, Chris. They had been best friends ever since playgroup, so had Ben and Jack, but Ryan and Chris were bullies and bullied everyone in the school.

One day, Ben and Jack were going to put a stop to this behaviour by getting back at Ryan and Chris. Ryan and Chris were getting people into trouble - like last week when Ryan broke a little girl's bike and made her cry, they ran off laughing their heads off and now Ben and Jack had to bump into them. 'What do you want, Ryan,' Ben said sarcastically.

Suddenly, Lavender came up behind Ryan and Chris and whispered something in their ears. Ben thought he knew what she said because suddenly, Ryan and Chris flew at Ben and Jack rapidly and took them to the floor. Five minutes later Ben woke up, so did Jack and they got up. Ryan and Chris had gone, with Lavender as well. 'Sheesh, I know she is your ex-girlfriend, but that was mean,' said Jack.
'Shut up,' Ben said.

Suddenly, Ben felt a pain. He knew the pain, it had killed him once before. He knew what was going to happen, he would shrink into his boots and would suck in the nearest person to kill him. Firstly, Ben's head shrank into his body and his body shrank into his legs and his legs shrank into his knees and his knees shrank into his boots and, surprised, Jack got sucked into the boots and the boots disappeared.

Benjamin Chaffe (10)
Westfield Junior School

The Graveyard

On the 1st of May, Jade Granger had a birthday party with her best friends and she had a sleep-over. Jade's friends dared her to go to the most haunted graveyard in the whole town, so she went and at this time, it was 3:00am. She went into the darkest place, suddenly something ran past her. Behind her, she heard the leaves and there were footsteps. Her heart felt like it had stopped, she couldn't move. After about twenty seconds, she ran and ran until she got home and told her friends all about it, then they went to sleep.

In the morning, she did what she normally did. The paper came and the front page said, 'People Disappearing!' so she went to call on her best friend called Jo Cox. She asked her to come with her to the graveyard, to call for her other friends, but she wasn't there.

Jade had just remembered the newspaper and told Jo. They decided to go into the graveyard at 3:00am again and find out what the thing was. Jade met Jo at the graveyard gates. Very slowly, they walked into the graveyard. 'What was that?' said Jo, her voice trembling.
'I have no idea, but that's what I heard before. Let's go!' said Jade, her voice trembling too.
'No, I want to find out what it is!' shouted Jo.
Suddenly, this huge, black thing came out in front of them. 'Arrghhhh!' they both screamed. Jo ran, but Jade stood still and couldn't run. Suddenly, the thing came closer and ate her. Now she haunts the graveyard on the first of May, all day and night.

Hayley Cannon (10)
Westfield Junior School

VIRUS BATTLE

One dull, miserable winter's day, Daniel Smith and Ehren Mountain-Chambers were on their way to Argos to buy two new Virus watches. Daniel is short, fast, strong, intelligent, has ginger hair and blue/green eyes. They both decided to get a different type of Virus watch. Daniel Smith a silver watch and Ehren Mountain-Chambers a black watch. Daniel decided to check out his watch. 'Hey Ehren, want a game from the silver watch?' said Daniel.
'Yeah, why not!' answered Ehren.
'OK, put your watch on receive . . . now!' said Daniel.

Teleportation appeared on both boys' watches. 'What does that mean?' they both screamed together.

They were being sucked into their watches. 'Help!' they screamed.
'What's that sound?' Daniel said, afraid.
'How should I know?' said Ehren, also afraid.
The sound was trumpets on the march and guns joined in as the sound came closer. It was on both sides. There was a captain from each team, one silver, one black. The silver captain boomed, 'Choose a team please, to settle this battle of virus watches!' then finally stopped.
'One to a team, OK!' boomed the black captain.
'I'll go on the black team then!' said Ehren.
'That means I've got to go on the silver team!' said Daniel.

As the battle raged on, the silver team seemed to be winning and suddenly, Daniel felt something cold on his wrists. At the other end of the battlefield, Ehren felt the same and then they both saw some bars. The next second, they were in jail, but were they . . ?

Daniel Mountain-Chambers (10)
Westfield Junior School

THE HAUNTED HOUSE

'Hi, I'm Jo and this is Jan.'

'Hiya!'

'We're both tomboys. I've got very short blonde hair and blue eyes.'

'Yeah, and I've got shortish brown hair and brown eyes.'

As you can see by now, we're best friends.

Anyway, Jan and I were going through the woods at night and it was really spooky. We found an old house. Jan said to me, 'Go on Jo, I dare you to go inside.'

'Um . . . OK,' I said.

I stepped up to the door and went for the door handle. I opened it slowly and stepped in. I trod on a trapdoor and fell down it. Jan ran over and said, 'Oh no, wait up!' She jumped down and landed on a soft, bouncy mat, but there was a long, long slide and suddenly we saw . . . a zombie, who held a sword. The zombie started to move and it chased us with the sword. We jumped up and slid down the slide. 'That was a close shave!' said Jan.

'Yeah, he nearly chopped off my head!' I joked.

Emily McGregor (10)
Westfield Junior School

The Revenge Of Lubu

One cold, windy night, the sun had set and six friends were walking on their way home from a paintball match. They had won the match and had lots of ammo left. They were walking past the cemetery, ten minutes away from their houses, when suddenly, the cemetery gate swung open.

Will said, 'Let's go in.'

He's a small, blonde-haired boy and quite brave, so they all went in. suddenly, the gate shut, 'What the . . ?' I said.

An arrow shot past Will's face and stuck into the tree's bark. A note flapped down from the arrow. Will read it out loud, 'Disturb my sleep and die.'

Liam pulled out his paintball gun and loaded it. Peter, Sean and Liam walked to the front door of the cemetery. Suddenly, they fell down a trapdoor. Will jumped and grabbed Liam's hand. 'Here, take my gun,' said Liam, and he let go to fall into the black hole. Tom and Ryan pulled out their guns and shot the door. It fell down and shattered on the ground. They jumped over the hole and went in. three ninjas jumped out of nowhere.

'I told you,' said a voice, it seemed to come from the walls. 'How are you . . ?'

William Winson-Pearce (10)
Westfield Junior School

THE DISAPPEARING GHOST

Once there were two boys called Josh and Tom. They went to Westfield Junior School. They were walking home and heard weird noises. They got scared. 'Tom, let's go this way, it's creepy,' said Josh worriedly.
'Let's go back to school,' Tom replied.
They ran back to school. On the way, they heard dogs barking and leaves crackling underneath their feet and it smelt nearly as revolting as a dead, rotten fish. 'Yes, we're back,' said Tom, relieved. They both were, but not for long. There was a man with blond frizzy hair, a white T-shirt with a black business shirt and trousers. There was only one problem, he had no face and there was a funny smell.
'Tom, stay still,' Josh whispered.
Tom was frozen solid, not blinking, he had all eyes on the ghost. Both of them were watching the ghost. The ghost was disappearing, all of it had disappeared except the head, in one second, that vanished.

They wandered around the school, noises started and things collapsed.
'Josh, the ghost's back,' said Tom worriedly.
'Hey! You, ghost!'
'What?' the ghost said.
'What do you want?'
'I want to know what happened to the 1965 Prime Minister. I was his guard.'
'He's dead.'
The ghost wept and disappeared, so Josh and tom spent the weekend happily!

Josh John (10)
Westfield Junior School

News Today

'Hello all viewers, welcome to World Today. We have some fascinating news, but absolutely disgusting. Just yesterday at the burger palace, a dreadful thing happened . . .'

'Here, I'll pass you over to Kent Highway.'

'Thanks John. Yesterday, young Jennifer Roads went in there for her tenth birthday. Jane, her mum, took her there. Once they were seated, they ordered two of the most famous McChicken burgers, with lettuce might I add. Jennifer and her mum got their favourite burgers and of course, Diet Pepsi. They were ready to eat, but when Jennifer bit into her delicious McBurger there was something rummaging ravenously through the lettuce. In that burger was, yes, it was . . . a *fly!* When her mum went to complain, the person who was serving her just said, 'The manager's out.'

So young Jenny's mum screamed, 'If you ever want us to come back here again, you'd better turn this joint around!'

There we have it folks, the story today. Back to John in the studio.'

'OK, now that was amazing folks. I'm sorry, that's all for today, goodbye for now.'

Hannah Mills (9)
Westfield Junior School

A SCARY STORY

Chris and Ryan were walking through the graveyard, rose bushes cutting their faces while they tore at their trousers. Suddenly, they made their way into a clearing, the starry night sky above them, the moonbeams glinting slightly on Chris's glasses, they crept through the church. *Ding! Ding!* The church bell rang, it was midnight. *Tap, tap.* Someone was following them, they knew for certain they were being followed because the someone or something was smoking.

Chris and Ryan stood still, petrified as the fresh scent of tobacco wafted over them. Ryan turned around, but there was nothing there! 'How strange,' remarked Chris.
They carried on walking, but stopped suddenly because an old, pudgy little man blocked their path. Ryan opened his mouth to speak, but the old man disappeared.

They finally got to the gate and Chris went to open it, but cut his hand on the rusty lock. Ryan brought out a penknife and he slashed at the rust, then they went through into the second part of the cemetery. With the gates not far, Chris and Ryan made a break for it and they went home.

Christopher Unwin (10)
Westfield Junior School

THE SECRETS

Hello, my name's Helen and I live in America. I've two friends, one's called Hannah and the other is Emily. I go to a school called New York High. I've got two enemies, Jamie and Edward, they try to split me, Emily and Hannah up.

'Hey, Hannah,' said Helen, 'wanna come to the park with me and Emily tonight?'
'All right then. Anyway, it will give us a chance to get away from Edward,' said Hannah, in a laughing sort of way.
Jamie heard all this, so he decided to go and tell Edward to go to the local park and play a trick on them. 'Edward, we need to go to the park tonight to play a wonderful trick on the girls,' whispered Jamie.
'OK then,' said Edward in his fashionable voice.

At 6:30pm, later that day, Emily, Hannah and Helen were at the park playing on the swings. Jamie came up behind them and said, 'I know a secret about Emily that you don't.'
'What is it?' said Hannah.
'She's kissed your boyfriend!'
Hannah jumped off the swing and threw Emily off hers. She tried to do a karate chop on Emily's arm and . . . *crack!* Hannah had broken Emily's arm! The boys gave their secret away by laughing. Hannah looked down at Emily and Emily was crying. She helped her up and plastered her arm for her and chased the boys into the woods. 'Sorry for not trusting you,' she said to Emily. They were all friends again.

Aaron Cohen-Gold (9)
Westfield Junior School

GHOST STORY

'Guess what?' Mandy said.

'What?' questioned Jessie.

Mandy was a sort of tomboy who always wore jeans and tops. Jessie was a tomboy too, she wore a baseball cap and trousers. They both had brown eyes and brown hair.

'I've got the key to my great, great, grandad's old house!'

'What, the haunted house?' Jessie said with a look of excitement in her eyes.

'Come on, let's go!' Mandy said.

So off they went. About ten minutes later, they were there. The house looked creepy and a bit lop-sided. 'Let's go in,' whispered Jessie. They went in, all the windows were broken and there were cobwebs all over.

'Hey, look over here,' Mandy said. There was a chest, in torchlight they reached for the buckle which was easy to open, then a *bang*. They both looked at each other.

Then a voice said, 'Hello!'

Mandy turned off the torch and Jessie grabbed the things in the chest, the things were soft and squidgy. Mandy grabbed Jessie, 'C'mon.'

They ran out, there was a car. Everything was pitch-black at first, but when the car's headlights went on, they got caught. Mandy was looking down at what Jessie had in her hand. 'What did you pick up from the chest, Jessie?' she said. As Jessie looked down, she saw three teddies in her hand.

'Um, they're teddy bears!' she said, laughing.

'Hey Mandy, that's your dad's car, isn't it?' Jessie said.

'That means that was your mum we ran away from!' she said, as they were laughing and laughing.

Kiri Storey (10)
Westfield Junior School

GHOST FOR HARRY POTTER

Harry, Hermione and Ron all arrived at Hogwarts. They went into the hall and had tea, then they went up to their house and sat around the fire. They heard a stomp. 'What's that noise?'

'I don't know,' said Hermione, 'but we'd better get our wands.'

It was getting louder and louder and louder, until they screamed. It was a dragon from Mayneer, but the dragon was ten metres taller than he was before. Harry said it was a bit obvious that the dragon was. Hagrid remembered now, 'It's an adult.' The dragon had been in a cave for forty years.

Ron went to the library. It was the day when they went to get new wands. They flew on their brooms - magic! The dragon was asleep in the dungeon. Professor McGonigall was teaching the class handwriting. She asked if they'd seen Harry, Ron or Hermione. She knew they were probably on some sort of adventure. She saw the dragon and pretended she was sick, so she had to go to the doctors! Oh, Harry!

Sophie Wood (9)
Westfield Junior School

THE EXCHANGE

Here we go again, same every year. Up to the attic I go - I wonder where it'll take me this time? There she was, my mum's old, sparkling time machine, Betsy. I carefully stepped inside and for some reason, without me pressing any buttons, I felt myself whizzing through time. I thought I was going to be sick.

Suddenly, the whizzing came to a stop. I opened Betsy's door. I could see a Victorian Market. Betsy spoke to me! I've never heard her speak before, I was taken aback. 'You're in the right time, but wrong place!' Suddenly, I was in a Victorian house with a family which was running around, shouting, 'James!'
'Who are you?' asked a girl.
'I'm ... um ... my name's Laura!' I said worriedly.
'Oh, have you found James?'
'Sorry, I haven't.'
Suddenly, I began to realise what had happened. For me to go back in time, someone had to go forward in time. That person must be James. The girl began to explain, 'James is my baby brother.' Then I told her what I thought. She gasped and cried, 'He'll die!'
'I know!' I exclaimed.
The girl pointed to a rug on the floor, 'You can sleep there!'

Breakfast was stale bread. The family hadn't woken up, but I ran and got in Betsy. We zoomed off and within two secs we were in 2002. I collected the baby and he was back to his home in the 1850s again. I can't wait till 2003!

Chloe Andrews (10)
Westfield Junior School

A DAY IN THE LIFE OF MY HEADTEACHER

At 6:00am, early on a Tuesday morning, Mr Burgess wakes up then gets dressed into his office suit, has his breakfast which is normally a slice of bread, or if he's lucky, two slices of toast. Next, he jumps into his car and sets off to school.

When he gets there, he goes into his office and signs some forms before school starts. He needs to rush to teach his maths group, I'm not sure he's ever early after all.

After all that, it's time for assembly. He goes in about five minutes earlier to get it ready, now he starts assembly. In assembly, he plays his noisy guitar which drives me crazy. After assembly finishes, he strolls into the staff room and scoffs down a whole bowl of jelly beans. Luckily, he has eaten them all before the bell goes for the children to come in from playtime. Then, he collects his detention book and goes and gives out some detentions, which makes him feel happy at the end of the day!

After all that, he has his lunch. Next, he will go and check that everyone is behaving and does that mostly for the rest of the afternoon.

At the end of the day, he goes home for dinner and to bed.

Sophie Banks (10)
Westfield Junior School

A DAY IN THE LIFE OF ME

8:30am I have just woken up, it is Saturday. I lay in bed till 10:20am, then I hear my alarm go off. I get out of bed and hear banging. I put my dressing gown on and open my door. I look outside my door and I can see John putting up tiles. 'Hello, Sam,' John says.
'Hello,' I say.

I walk down the stairs, Dad is already dressed, so I go into the lounge and switch on the television. It's Sabrina, The Teenage Witch. I sit down and put a big, blue blanket over me. Then, when the episode is finished, I go upstairs and have a shower. The water is hot as it sprays on my arms and legs.

I turn the shower off, get dressed, go over to Ruby's and play in the garden. Emma, Ruby's mum, goes to the park with Mary and Charlie. Ruby and I raid the sweet box. We go and eat them secretly and play in the garden for half an hour. Emma comes back, she cooks dinner. We eat it and I say, 'That was lovely, can I have some more?'
'No,' she says.

We have a choc-ice then. We play outside until seven o'clock, then I go home and read. Then it's time for bed. Zzzzzzzzz!

Samantha Ambler (10)
Westfield Junior School

ONE DEAD, TWO ALIVE
(Based on a true story)

OK, so there he was, *dead.* Mouth open, eyes open too. He had been hit by a lorry and was in the ditch. It was his birthday soon. Patch had gone missing the night before, he was a cat.

A few days passed and my mum picked me up from school. She seemed happy, but I wasn't, for my cat had just died. When I got home, my mum said, 'We have to go in the back door.'
Now I was suspicious. When I got in, my mum was looking behind the settee. Inside the house, I was about to go upstairs to cry, when I heard a miaow, and then again. I stepped closer to the settee. I saw a completely white kitten, with a bit of black. I named her Lucy.

I saw a dog called Lady, two years later and now I've got a new dog.

I'm now ten, and because of Patch, I've joined the Wood Green Young Supporters to help other animals, giving them a chance of life. Patch dying was bad, but now I'm helping other animals that have been rescued.

Emily-Jane Sparks (10)
Westfield Junior School

A DAY IN THE LIFE OF MY FRIEND

I woke up bright and early, then I got dressed. I had breakfast, it was Cinnamon Grahams and orange juice. Then I got washed. I hate washing. Made my bag for school and left to go to school.

I'm at school now, same as every day, dancing, screaming, shouting and throwing paper planes at the teacher while she is writing on the board. Suddenly, Mr Burgess stormed in, ranting and raving. 'Be quiet!' he bellows. 'You all have detention for a month!'
Luckily, I sneaked out of the room without anyone seeing me, until Mr Burgess worked out I was gone. He came out of the classroom, I ducked into the toilet. 'Jemma, Jemma, where are you little girl?' he shouted.
I stepped out of my hiding place, 'I needed the toilet, Mr Burgess,' I whimpered.
'OK then, Jemma,' Mr Burgess said.
He turned around and I ran up to him and kicked his bottom. I ran down the stairs and went home.

The next day at school, Mr Burgess couldn't sit down and I had another two weeks detention and my mum and dad shouted at me.

Jenna Spencer-Briggs (10)
Westfield Junior School

THE HEADLESS GHOST

One dark winter's night, I was fast asleep when suddenly I started dreaming about a headless ghost. It was a very tall ghost, about three metres tall. It was also very ugly. It wore a big, black cloak with silver stars on it.

It started to chase after me, I thought I would never get away, when suddenly I saw a house. It looked like a house out of a horror film. It leant to one side and it had broken windows, also one of its doors was hanging off one hinge. I quickly ran through the door.

I nearly choked, it smelt like rotten eggs and cheese. I looked behind me, the ghost was still chasing after me. I quickly ran up the stairs. As I stepped on each of the steps, they creaked. I went into one of the rooms. The room's walls were covered with spiders' webs and spiders. Then suddenly, out of the corner of my eye, I saw a trapdoor. I crept towards it, then I jumped in it. I had escaped.

Suddenly, I woke up. I turned on the light and there in the doorway was the headless ghost . . .

Jemma Yeowart (10)
Westfield Junior School

FRANKENSTEIN IN THE FRIDGE

Jemma had a long day. She went to bed early. She woke up because there was a thunderstorm. She went to get a glass of milk. Jemma opened the fridge to get some milk and when she did, a Frankenstein popped out. She went to tell her mum and dad, but they would not believe her. The Frankenstein chased her in and out of rooms, upstairs and downstairs. Her mum told her to be quiet, because Jemma was making a lot of noise. Suddenly, the Frankenstein ran downstairs and got back in the fridge. He shut the door with a *bang!* When she opened the door, the Frankenstein had disappeared. Jemma was freaked out. Her mum and dad were cross because they didn't get any sleep!

Lucy Jones (10)
Westfield Junior School

THE DAY WHEN THE ALIENS TRIED TO TAKE OVER THE WORLD

Once upon a time, there was a girl called Samantha. She was on her way back from the park when she saw lots of aliens. They were standing next to their spaceship arguing. Samantha had brown hair, as brown as chocolate and her eyes were as blue as a cloudless sky.

The next day, she went back to the same place. She saw the aliens and they were still standing there arguing. Suddenly, she was caught, she screamed and ran. The aliens started to run after her. Suddenly, she stopped running and turned around. Out of nowhere, she pulled a laser gun from her pocket and said, 'Hasta la vista, baby.' She fired the gun. Suddenly, the aliens blew up and all this green goo landed on her. Samantha went around picking up bits of their bodies. Then she started walking home.

When she got home, her mum said, 'What have you been up to?'
Samantha said, 'Oh, nothing much. Just stopped aliens from taking over the world!'

Ruby Pratt (9)
Westfield Junior School

A Day In The Life Of My Mum And I

At 8:00am, Pete, Samantha's dad, woke me up with a big shake. I had a bath and got dressed. Then Debbie, Samantha's mum, took me to my nana's house. I reminded Nana that I was going to see Atomic Kitten live at the Hammersmith Apollo.

At 9:00am, my mum and I went on a train to London. Mum and I couldn't find our hotel, so we asked where our hotel was. The person we asked told us a long way, but it was just up the road. When we found the hotel, it was a five star hotel. It was called The Jury. We went to a museum, it was massive.

At 7:30pm we got ready. When we got to the Hammersmith Apollo there wasn't a long queue. There were cat faces on the wall and the crowd's faces looked very excited. When I came out after the concert, Mum and I went back to the hotel and got room service. I fell asleep, and on Tuesday, we came back to St Ives.

Chloe Ackerlay (10)
Westfield Junior School

THE B TEAM

The laboratory was the hideout of The B Team and their leader, Mr B. Perhaps you'd like me to say the name and description of Mr B?

Mr B is the leader, he's tall and strong. He has a hair cut like a cross, his skin is white and black, his eyes are as blue as the sky on a nice summer's day. Mr B wears gold boots, blue shorts and a silver-green T-shirt.

The rest of the team are called Rabbit, Sgt Tiger, Pepper Facer, Boxing Machine, Rhino Whip and Slaughter Man.

Rhino Whip and Pepper Facer found a tunnel that led to King Monkey's hideout. It was called Wuuu Zoo. His crime partner was Queen Tigress.
'Ah, there's nothing like crime,' said King Monkey.
'Absolutely,' said Queen Tigress.
It wasn't long before the B Team arrived.
'Imposters!' said King Monkey. 'Queen Tigress destroy them.'
Boxing Machine pulled out his bomb and before long, queen Tigress and King Monkey were taken to jail. However, the B Team, Mr B and the gang celebrated their victory against King Monkey and Queen Tigress.

Samuel Weston (10)
Westfield Junior School

A DAY IN THE LIFE OF SAMMY KAY

Sammy Kay is a very kind 10-year-old girl who does lots of things. She has eyes like a brown cornfield and her hair is like chocolate. She does lots of activities in one day. She has to get ready early in the morning to go swimming and then get back in time for school at 9:00am. Then, after school she does drama, which she really likes. Her teacher is called Mike.

After that, Sammy goes to Brownies, she really likes this. Her leader is called Sarah. Also she does ballet and her ballet teacher is called Amy. She also does modern dance, she is also really fond of this. Her teacher is called Rebecca for that. Sammy says she is really nice.

Afterwards, she goes home to have her tea. Then she goes to bed to have a rest after a long day doing all her clubs.

Stacey Fletcher (10)
Westfield Junior School

A Day In The Life Of Danny The Dog

Danny has breakfast, takes a walk round the garden, has a second helping of breakfast and sleeps. Then he wakes up, has lunch, makes a date with the pooch next door, and sleeps.

Later he wakes up, has tea, grooms himself and goes on his date. They go to a disco, they have lots of fun, have a big slice of cake and have bottles of beer.

He comes back from his date, bottle of beer in his paw, climbs on the sofa and sleeps!

Chantelle Keepin (9)
Westfield Junior School

MR BILL AND MR BOB, THE BUILDERS

It was a nice, sunny day in Mary Poppin land. Mr Bill and Mr Bob were asleep, until they got a call to build a railing over the well, so people can't fall in. Bob and Bill got dressed and drove to the well.

They got to the well and started to build and Mr Bill fell in, but luckily he did not hurt himself. Bob thought quickly and went to get Crainy. Crainy lifted Mr Bill out. Then they finished the work and went home to sit in their chairs and have a cup of tea. One hour later, they went to bed.

The next day, they had to build a shed. It all went well and they finished the work. They went home and went to sleep.

Peter Cox (10)
Westfield Junior School

THE NIGHT OF THE LIVING DEAD

It was Hallowe'en, I went to the graveyard to visit my dad's grave. The clock struck twelve, these hands stuck out of the grave, the trees waved, the gravestone started moving. I was terrified. My two best friends, Mehmet and Sam, were standing behind me.

We hid behind my dad's grave, we heard their plan to take over the world. We stood there listening. Their first attack was to take over the school.

We ran and the zombies must have heard us, because they started to chase us so we ran faster. We though of what we could do. Mehmet said, 'The vacuum cleaner on backwards would blow out and if we hoovered up stakes, that would kill the zombies.'
'Yeah! That's what we're going to do!' I said.
It worked.

Luke Bird (10)
Westfield Junior School

A DAY IN THE LIFE OF BART SIMPSON

I get up and watch Itchy and Scratchy until school time, then I go to school on my skateboard. Our first lesson is spelling - I get nil. I have had a detention for putting rabbit diarrhoea in the teacher's desk. After that, we had a hard lesson about shapes, in which I mentioned a very rude word which I must not repeat, so I got another detention for that.

Next, I had a really boring history lesson. I fell asleep and had a weird dream, then I woke up and went home. After that, I watched Itchy and Scratchy until tea time. I had my tea, it was pizza, then I watched more Itchy and Scratchy and went to bed.

George Purvis (10)
Westfield Junior School

THE HORROR FROM HELL

I'm a 12-year-old boy with curled blond hair and dark, deep blue eyes. I'm wearing combat trousers and a white shirt. Anyway, I was on my way to my gran's house. She lived on a cliff edge. When I got there, I was tired and I needed a rest, so I climbed up the spiral staircase, up to my room. I fell asleep on the bed instantly. When I woke up, it was cold and dark. I looked at my watch, it was 11:38pm. I walked out of my room and a zombie launched itself at me and fell down the spiral staircase. I fell down the stairs too. I found myself in Hell and the ground fell through and landed in a boiling pool of lava. I woke up, it was a dream.

Kurt Noack (10)
Westfield Junior School

A DAY IN THE LIFE OF CATHERINE PRITCHARD

Catherine Pritchard has hair the colour of a cornfield, her eyes are the colour of chocolate. In the morning, Catherine gets up bright and early, ready for swimming. Catherine gets in the car and her mum, Debbie, takes her to the recreation centre to do swimming.

Catherine got into the water, it was *freezing!* When Catherine quickly got out, she rushed home, had a piece of toast and got to school for nine o'clock. Catherine's teacher was in a big mood. She made the whole class have detention.

After school, Catherine went to ballet, but she forgot that it was the teacher's day off. By this time, Catherine was getting tired. Catherine didn't want to go to hockey, but her mum dragged her up to the ice rink. By this time, Catherine just wanted to go to bed. At modern, she forgot her shoes so she had to sit out. When she went to tap, she forgot the dance, so the teacher had to go all through it again. Then at last, she got home pooped and fell straight to sleep ready for the next day.

Sammy Kay (9)
Westfield Junior School

WORLD WAR II

Commander Ammo was in the war rushing through, when a bomb exploded nearby, knocking Commander Ammo to the ground and out. He woke up in a German hospital. As his eyes began to see again, he saw a German leaning over him. He whispered, 'I'm not a German. I'm English and I'm an under cover as a German, my name's Peter.' He radioed the field hospital and Commander Ammo was rescued. Three hours later, he was in the field hospital, getting better by the minute.

Aydn Reece (10)
Westfield Junior School

My Holiday To Hollywood

Here we are at the airport. I am so excited, this is the first ever holiday with my friends. We are going to *Hollywood*, yes! My friends are Beth, Lauren, Rajane, Sophie and Lisette. It takes twenty-four hours to get to Hollywood in a plane. I am leaving with my friends at 10:00am . . .
Must be off, it's 10:00am. Come on you guys, don't want to miss the plane.

When we were in the plane, we were reading pop magazines and having girly chats. Twenty-four hours later we were there at Hollywood. The first thing I did was unpack my clothes, then me and my friends went to go and have fun. We went to the beach and we went to have something to eat. We went to a theme park too. After that, we went to see famous pop stars. We tried rock climbing, and fell off! I had to go to hospital straight away. When I was in hospital, my friends came to see me, 'Are you alright?' said Beth.
'Yes,' I said, joyfully. 'I'll be going home tomorrow.'
'Cool. Here's your chocolates.'
'Thanks, and for the flowers. Hey, there's some chocolates missing!'
'Sorry!' said Lisette.

I won't forget the holiday to Hollywood ever!

Charlotte Hood (10)
Westfield Junior School

A BOY

Once there was a boy, a boy who never thought that he would be popular; the king of the schools. This boy was called Rob, he never wanted to be cool until he got a bit of a beating. He was smashed up against the wall until his hands were covered in blood. When he got home, Rob went to his room and thought about being popular.

The next day, he went shopping for the coolest clothes in the world, so they had to fly to America. They stayed there for a bit and came back when they were needed. Rob and his mum came back after three years, and Rob was the king of the schools. He bullied, he stole and he played footy.

One day it all went wrong, when Max came. He was the king of the schools. He beat Rob at footy, he stole from Rob and he bullied Rob. Rob knew it was the end of his cool life. Rob is called, 'Rob the snob.' He will never have fun again because he bullied, stole and was nasty.

Santino Zicchi (10)
Westfield Junior School

KATE'S YEARS OF BECOMING A HERO

One sunny day, Kate's parents were bundling outside to find Ryan in a wheelchair, but home for good. Kate was wondering what all the noise was about. She came out and found Ryan, but she didn't walk up to Ryan. Instead, she walked up to the postman and asked, 'Is there a letter for me?'

The postman replied, 'Yes, are you Kate Bail?'

'Yes, I am.'

Kate opened the letter and it said she had been accepted into King's Bun Hospital. But there was one problem, even though she had got the job, Ryan was home now, so she wouldn't be able to treat him, only in check ups. Two years passed and Kate had become a fully-trained nurse. She helped her brother at home get more confident at walking. The other day, she was called in and saved a man's life when he had a heart attack. Kate became another King's Bun Hospital Hero! They were the best years ever.

Courtney Woodrow (10)
Westfield Junior School

THREE CHILDREN, ONE MAN

I woke up. My leg was hurting a little because yesterday, I nearly broke it. The reason why is because a bullet went banging into it. I sat up and tried to climb out of bed without hurting it even more. I managed to climb out of bed, I balanced myself, then I stumbled over to the window. It looked dark and gloomy. Well, old places which look like a house on fire do. I looked back across the room. On the floor lay Mary-Grace and Peter. I found them in a train tube yesterday sitting next to their mum, screaming for help. I would have felt heartless if I left them there, so I took them back with me. They started to scream even more, because they thought I was the man who killed their mum. I helped them to my house, well I couldn't say it's a house, it's more like a barn, burnt down. I hoped no one would find us here.

All of a sudden, an aircraft carrier was firing through the window. I screamed, but realised that there were children here with me. I moved my way through the smelly old metal and saw Peter's leg, half missing. He was screaming so loudly. Then I heard men's voices. I looked behind me, there were more men dying, some dead. I looked back round to see . . . it had gone quiet. I put my fingers on Peter's neck, there was no pulse. Peter was dead.

All of a sudden, two men came and swiped Mary-Grace. They jumped out of the window. 'Nooo!' I screamed.
They were gone.

Jade Hannah (10)
Westfield Junior School

DOUBLE TROUBLE TWINS

It was a nice, bright, sunny day when I set off to Camp Walden for a year. My twin sister Chloe was with me. My mum, Sarah, and my dad, Nick, had split up when I was a baby. My mum lives in London and my dad lives in a hotel in New York. I live with my mum and Chloe lives with my dad.

I have a little cabin with my best friend called Sarah and our cabin is called Super Duper Looper. I miss my dad a lot, but I have one photo of him. Enough about me, let's get on about the rooms. We have a big dinner room and a craft room and one big, massive lounge.

Guess what happened yesterday? I went to my friend's house and she has one big heck of a dog called Winny and she bit me on my leg and arm. The next day, I went into hospital to get it checked out. It was bruised and I had to have twenty stitches. The worst part was that I was never allowed to go out, because the air would get to it and it would go very red and it was very painful. Chloe could feel her arm and leg hurting too, even though Winny bit *me*.

Henna Hussain (10)
Westfield Junior School

THE WRESTLING PRINCESS

Hiya, (or to all you posh folk, hello) my name is Kit (the princess). I am going to tell you all about me, and this bonehead of a prince, Kot. Kot was always saying I was a real girly-girl princess, that I couldn't even lift an apple and if I started crying, he would call me a cry baby. But I am in no way like that. I can wrestle lions and stuff, and I am really independent too, so boys, even though I'm pretty, lay off!

He shouldn't have called me a girly-girl because I would get really mad ... and I did. So I challenged him to a wrestling match and he said, 'Yeah, sure. I could do that with my hands behind my back.' He was showing off as usual.
But I knew he couldn't so I told him to have his hands behind his back. He said moodily, 'it's not fair.'
So we had the match (he was struggling *sooooo* much) and guess who won? Me!

He demanded a rematch, so I gave him one. (He didn't have his hands behind his back that time.) Guess who won? Me! Ha!

Who's the strongest now? Me!

Rajane Kaur (10)
Westfield Junior School

Maris's Dream

It was ten o'clock and Maris was heading upstairs for bed. Maris got into bed and set the alarm for 7:10am. Slowly, she drifted off to sleep. That night, Maris had a strange dream. She was sitting watching a movie, only it wasn't a movie, it was real life. It was a battle between the elves and the trogs who were worst enemies. She watched transfixed, then, as Santino the leader was about to kill her father, she screamed, 'Noooo!' Then she woke up.

The next morning, she went to see her best friend, Tom. Maris explained her dream while Tom listened with bated breath. 'Do you know what it means?' Maris asked.
'I don't know, I'm not a fortune teller,' Tom said shakily. 'What was that?'
An explosion seemed to have taken place nearby. They ran to find out. 'Oh my,' exclaimed Maris. It was the battle from her dream. Then without warning, the blue and green elves blood drenched them, an elf had been killed. Then, without thinking, Maris seized her dead father's sword, swung it high over her head and brought it down with a *crack* over the head of Santino. From then on, Maris was a heroine. It was unlikely the trogs would ever come back.

Sarah Luxon (10)
Westfield Junior School

THE BURNED FOREST

Long ago in the misty morning, Vicky and Bill woke up.
'It's time,' said Bill.
'Time for what?' said Vicky.
'Time to explore the forest,' replied Bill.
'You know I'm scared of that forest!' screamed Vicky.
With this, Vicky pulled the covers over her head.

After they had their breakfast, Bill asked Vicky if she was coming to the forest.
'Yes,' said Vicky. With that, Vicky and Bill rushed upstairs, got changed and rushed out of the house. They walked for what seemed hours. Finally, they got to the forest. They entered the forest. To their disgust, all the trees were burned.
'What's happened to the trees?' said Vicky.
Bill didn't have time to answer, for there was a massive dragon chasing them. Vicky and Bill ran up the tree, the dragon was waiting at the bottom of the tree.
'I've got a plan,' said Vicky. 'I've got a mirror and you have got a belt. Can you give me your belt?'
Vicky tied the two things together and put them down the tree. The dragon blew some fire. The fire bounced on the mirror and blew up the dragon. They never went to the forest again.

Sophie Raine (10)
Westfield Junior School

MENTAL DRIVER

Once in the heart of America, there was a hotel. In one of the rooms, there were five robbers and they were all planning out a robbery at the jewellery shop on the other side of town. If they were going to get there, they would have to hurry up, so they got into the car and whizzed off.

About a quarter of the journey in, a cop chased them. They did not panic 'cause the slip road to the motorway was nearby. They went up the slip road and travelled a mile, when they came to a hole in the side of the road.

They swerved over to it and the cop car followed and ran right through the hole. The bad guys put the gearbox in reverse, thinking that it was in first. They went into the hole and got caught!

Adam Cash (10)
Westfield Junior School

WAR

It's ten-past one in the afternoon and guns are going off one by one. People are falling dead every second. You're holding your finger down on a trigger and all you can hear is cries for help and screaming in pain, and you're pulling on a trigger. All you can see is orange dust and you can't breathe properly because of the humid conditions. Then, your friend next to you falls on the ground. You run and run as every man falls dead on the ground. You climb down a hole and see screaming men begging for treatment, full grown men crying their hearts out, and others lying there dead. You go back up the hole and see more men holding a trigger and all you can hear is *thump* where bodies are falling dead on the ground. Then you look up and there's a plane with its propellers going round, then, something gets pushed out of the back of the plane. You jump back and fall over, you get up and run, run as fast as you can. But there's not use, as it explodes! So you collapse, relieved that you have died. You close your eyes for the final time.

Joel Marshall (10)
Westfield Junior School

THE RETURN OF GODZILLA

It was 7pm at night and it was quiet in New York. Then something extraordinary happened. It was Godzilla. He was angry because they'd killed his mother. Godzilla hit a building down and it went everywhere. People tried to run away and tried not to be squashed. It was horrific. People were getting squashed and cars were getting blown up, the rubble was hitting the cars. Meanwhile, while this mayhem was happening, Godzilla was running back into the sea.

The next morning, three cops were called. There names were Officer Marshall, Officer Polvere and Officer Parker. They were all professional cops. They had been cops for two years and they knew where Godzilla was hiding. So they got in their submarine and went to try and find Godzilla.

They found him in the sewers. Officer Marshall shot him in the leg and the arm, then Officer Polvere shot him in his other leg and arm. Officer Parker shot him in the head, but Godzilla made them all bleed by swiping at them. It took 1,000 people to carry Godzilla back into the sea.

Liam Parker (10)
Westfield Junior School

FATHER, SON AND A SECRET

This is a story about me and how I was a hero, but enough about me.

Well, after dinner, my mum called out to me and shouted, 'tom, could you put out the trash, sugar plum!'
I hate it when she calls me that. Oh by the way, my name is Tom, Tom Right. Carrying on with the story; I went down to the street outside our back gate and then to my surprise, a spaceship was in the road. I saw a bright green light, then I woke up in a prison. I was shaking all over, so scared I couldn't move. Then a man walked in, he sat inn front of me and said, 'You are the Prince of Evil, my son,' as he put up his hand and he put his fingers down, except his thumb and little finger. 'This is our father and son secret sign,' he said and he put the finger sign on my head and said, 'I'm coming home.'

I woke up back in my bed, with my mum shouting, 'He's alive and your dad's here. He's come back home.'
'I found you last night, outside!'
I looked up at my dad and he smiled, put up the secret sign and I knew he was the one who saved me the night before. It would be our secret forever . . .

Lisette Cook (10)
Westfield Junior School

The Man Who Lived

One day, a man named John Thompson, a professor, got up at seven o'clock to start work on his time machine. He finished at 5pm the next afternoon. He went to test it out, heart thumping louder and louder as he got nearer to the machine. Hand on the door handle, he thought 'What if it works? What if I get transported to the future? I haven't worked out all the bugs yet. I'll put my brain in gear.'

John ran into the library to find 'Transport Matters'. He ran the name of the book over and over in his mind. 'Here it is,' he said to himself.

John looked on the books on transporting bugs. He looked up *electrocharge* and as he said to himself he realised he had already invented it. 'Brilliant,' he said.
While John was shooting the time machine with the electro-charge gun, a computer chip came flying out. It was fried.

John went into the machine and turned it on. He heard a swirling noise, and when the swirling noise finished, John got out of the machine to see that the world had been destroyed. John went back in time to tell the president. He got back to 2002 to tell everyone. 'Mr President, Mr President, the world is going to be over soon. I went to 2037 and there was nothing there.'
Then the president said, 'What was it?'
'A pollution blast I think,' replied John.
The president said, 'Tell every car firm to shut down.'

Two years later, John warned the president, 'It should begin at three o'clock this afternoon. Mr President . . . It's time, Mr President,' John said. At ten minutes past three, nothing had happened. The world was saved.

Jacob Hawkins (10)
Westfield Junior School

THE MAGIC BIRTHDAY

It was my birthday and we were all going to London for the day. All my friends came up and we all set off. When we got out of the train, we went straight in. Me and my best friend Holly were first in the pool. The rest of them a few minutes later.

First we went diving, then we all ran up the stairs to the slide. I was first, everyone else was watching me. When I got to the bottom, I couldn't see anything, it was pitch-black. My friends couldn't see me, I had disappeared to Disneyland. I was on the roller coaster hanging upside down, it was broken. Everyone else was rushing down the slide to find me, one by one they arrived on the roller coaster. By now, we were screaming our heads off. We were stuck there for half an hour.

We went on another roller coaster ride that lasted twenty-five minutes. We were queuing up for the water slide when we couldn't see anything but black, and we were back in the pool again. We all got out and went back home, then everyone said how good the party was!

Hannah Dale (10)
Westfield Junior School

THE ROCKET LAUNCH

One gloomy, windy day in America's rocket launch base, Sunday, June 26th, the rocket Seal Team 10 were setting up an extraordinary rocket launch. The team have been doing this rocket launch for ages, more than a year now. The two brave men, Paul who has been on one moon mission, aged 28, and finally the captain, Tony, who has been on five missions and has been captain on all five of them, are the crew.

The next day, they were walking to the rocket with loads of heavy white gear, food and pictures of their family to remember them by, because they would be up there for a long time.

'Five, four, three, two, one . . . we have lift-off!' shouted the captain of Seal Team 10. 'Give us a wave, Tony,' said the captain. Joyfully, Tony gave them a wave and then cut the line off the base. They were heading for the moon when the controls went all funny. 'Mayday, Mayday,' cried Tony.
They were heading straight for Jupiter and were just about to hit . . .

Giuseppe Polvere (10)
Westfield Junior School

THE FIGHT

One day on the planet Sandtom, a girl called Molly and her mum, Candoa, were sitting in their stable watching TV on a pile of hay. They were watching Graba (the channel where they have to watch because if their number was picked out of the hat, they would be Graba's slaves). Candoa was 5291 and Molly was 795862 and the number today was 5291. 'Noooo!' shouted Candoa as she was beamed up.

Then Tebathon and Frisco, the builders, came in and said, 'We will get your mum back,' and they drew out their swords.
They flew around the world and got into the spaceship and saw Candoa trying to escape, so they hid. They saw Graba's army capture Candoa. 'No!' screamed Molly as they took her away.
'Now you know what's going to happen,' whispered Frisco.
They smashed through the window and jumped and got onto the craft with Candoa on. The craft slowly hovered over the Sand Of Death (a hole in the sand). Frisco and Tebathon drew out their swords and started killing everyone except Candoa. When all the killing was done, they took Candoa back to Molly. 'Mum!' she said, and they all lived happily ever after.

Matthew Davis (10)
Westfield Junior School

MY BIRTHDAY

I woke up with a real buzz. Today was the day of my tenth birthday party. I didn't waste any time, I got up and got ready. About five minutes later, the whole house was up and ready. It was 8 o'clock and I was raring to go, then I realised my friends didn't come until 11 o'clock. I thought I was going to burst! The three hours seemed to last forever, with my excitement building and the hours going by, I couldn't wait!

It was five to eleven and my first friend arrived. Rajane was as excited as me, then my second friend arrived, Hannah. Then my mum told me something that delayed my excitement for a split second. They couldn't all come with us, some of them were making their own way there, but that didn't matter, so at about 11:30, me and my friends set off to the bowling alley.

At 1 o'clock, we all sat down and ate (although we got told off for being too loud!) We went back to my house for cake, and all in all, I had a brilliant day. I think my friends did too, or so they said!

Alphie Burgess (10)
Westfield Junior School

THE ANT CATASTROPHE

Hermione Grainger was reading a book in her bedroom, when she heard a squeak. She turned to look at her ant farm. 'Oh, you ants,' she said, 'what are you whinging for?' They stopped immediately.

The next day, Hermione got a weird package. Ant food. She asked herself, 'I wonder why I got that?' She fed the ants the food and they seemed to like it, but it made them grow absolutely enormous, until one day, the ants burst out of their tank. Hermione didn't know because she was asleep, but she woke up, a startled look on her face. She could hear petrified screams. She looked out of her window where people were crying, 'Hermione, get your wand out!'
So Hermione cried, 'Lumos holem!'

The ants carried on staying big, so they had to stay in their houses and couldn't come out until Hermione learnt a spell to shrink the ants.

Charlotte Goodwin (10)
Westfield Junior School

A Day In The Life Of A Sheep

I woke up. It was another hot, sunny day in the barn. How I hated that small pen Mr Biggle and Larry Biggle had given to me. 'A sheep should have a field, not a pen!' I said to myself. 'I have to escape!'
'You can't escape from her,' said Hubert, the old pig who had been listening.
'Don't listen to him,' shouted Quackers, the duck, 'you see that bar over there?'
'Yes,' I said, wondering what Quackers was on about.
'It's loose, just give it a quick push and you'll be free!'

I ran towards the bar and pushed it. Quackers was right! I ran out, bleating like mad. Mr Biggle and Larry heard me. They ran out as fast as they could, I dodged them this way and that, but they caught me. When I was back in my pen, I said to myself, 'Well, that was a nice bit of freedom, but I have to admit after all that dodging, I would rather stay in my pen. At least I get fed!'

I might try to escape some other time, but just for now, I think I'll stick to my pen!

Sarah Kinder (10)
Westfield Junior School

A DAY IN THE LIFE OF RYAN

Ryan walks in the front door to find one of his mates, Hannah.

'Hi, Ryan. What are you doing?' she said in a funny way, it sounded like a pig in a hut.

'Oh nothing, do you want to go to my room and play on the PlayStation?' he replied in an aggravating tone.

Ryan's room was full of Arsenal stuff. He had an Arsenal bed, and Arsenal watch; both he and Hannah liked the Gunners. Just then, the doorbell rang. It made Hannah jump out of her skin. It was Chris and Samantha. Hannah had a brill idea to go to the park and build a tree house.

Finally after four hours of hard work and slavery, the tree house was finished. Just then, Ryan heard a rumble, the tree house fell down.

'Where's Chris?' said Hannah in a worried way.

'Oww, my leg's broken. Get this tree house off me you der-brains!' said Chris.

So Ryan, Hannah and Samantha lifted the bits of the tree house off of Chris. But Hannah then heard a rumble, *smash!* A tree landed on Samantha.

'Oww, my neck! I think I have broken it.'

Hannah phoned an ambulance on her mobile phone. Samantha sadly died in the ambulance, but Chris was alright.

Ryan Hornett (10)
Westfield Junior School

GHOST STORY

Hi, I am Becky and here is my brother, Tom, the one with dark brown hair, thin lips, slightly wonky teeth and wide eyes. And me, I've got long blonde hair, shiny eyes, clean teeth. We have to stay at this massive hotel. It smells, it's creepy, dark and there are spiders' webs. Anyway, we are staying here, because my room caught on fire. I'm not sure how because I was at Brownies, so . . . wait a minute, my mum's calling me. 'Right Becky, I'm just going out to buy some food. You stay here.'

The second Mum had gone, I heard this noise. I asked Tom, 'What's that noise?'
'I can't hear anything,' Tom replied. 'Actually, now I hear something.'
I looked right and then left, but I didn't look behind me, so I did, shaking, and when I did, I saw a massive black thing. It had seven legs, no it had eight legs, four on each side.
Tom yelled, 'It's a huge spider. The spider is twice as big as my head!'
'I'm back,' called our mum.
'Mum, watch out!' screamed Tom as the spider was crawling towards her.
'Arghhh!' screeched our mum. 'Good news, we are moving house.'
'Yeah.'
'I know, I sorted it all out, so let's get in the car.'
'Wow! I love this house,' I said with amazement.
'Me too,' said Tom.
'And there's not any spiders either!' said Mum.

Catherine Pritchard (10)
Westfield Junior School

GHOST

I walked through the front door of the mansion, into a creepy hall, stairs on either side. There were lots of doors. Which one to choose? I went through a door that said, 'Enter if you dare.'

I entered and I saw an empty room, but there was a skeleton on the floor with a gun in its hand. There was a door ahead, I went through it. I saw a snake on the floor, ten metres long, and it was asleep.

I had to find my dad. I got the gun and shot the snake. I went through the next door, I saw my dad tied up and somebody about to shoot him. I shot him, untied my dad, then we ran away.

Rowan Staden (9)
Westfield Junior School

A Day In The Life Of . . .

Once upon a time, there was a little girl called Bekki (me!) and she lived with her parents, Emma and John and they all lived happily in a big house. But one day, Bekki was camping on a school trip and the weather was bad, really bad, and Bekki heard a scream outside. She ran to help a little girl, Amy, who was drowning in the river. She pulled Amy out of the water, then lightning struck in front of her face, so she fainted. She went blind in one eye because the lightning slashed her face. She woke up and stumbled back to the campsite. She heard on the radio that a lady was driving to pick up her daughter from camp, but in the wet weather, she had crashed into a signpost. The lady was called Emma Jones.

'Emma Jones, that's my mum,' Bekki said.

She ran and ran all the way to the car. 'My mum's car,' she said.

'Your mum was in that car?' said the policeman.

'Yes,' Bekki said.

'I am sorry, but your mum has passed away.' Said the lady.

Bekki started to cry. In her head was . . . the slam of brakes . . . a scream . . . silence . . .

Amelia Briggs (9)
Westfield Junior School

THE FORGOTTEN TREASURE OF THE GHOST HOUSE

One day, Paul and Connor were walking along. Paul was big, with brown eyes and blond hair. Connor was bigger, with blue eyes and brown hair. When they met Tom, he was slightly smaller than Connor, with brown eyes and brown hair. He dared Paul and Connor to break into the ghost house. So they went to the ghost house and broke in. They saw some rats for a second, then Connor saw something else. He walked over and grabbed something. He came back and said, 'Cool, a treasure map, it leads to treasure in the basement I think.'

They walked off with the map. Eventually they got to a table with swords and shields above it. Paul said to Connor, 'We're going to have to take a sword each, in case of danger.'
Paul grabbed a ruby encrusted sword, while Connor grabbed a diamond encrusted shield. Connor looked at the map. 'The door to the treasure is under the table.' They looked down and saw a trapdoor. They opened it and saw a little pile of gold and silver. They grabbed as much as they could.

Immediately, zombies and ghosts appeared. Connor's shield started to glow and so did Paul's sword. Connor rammed into the zombies with his shield and the zombies disappeared, so Paul did the same. They ran out of the house with the gold. They had escaped, stinking rich!

Paul Long (9)
Westfield Junior School

PADDY PAT'S REVENGE

One day I, Tom Howard and William were walking along on their way to the haunted house, because they had heard rumours that there where ghosts in there. I was fast and strong. Will was quick, nippy and smart. Will said to me, 'I'm sure Paddy Pat, The Dark Avenger, has got something to do with this.'
So when we reached the haunted house, the door automatically opened. We walked in, we went through another door. It was the kitchen. I saw a saucepan floating, I shot it with my gun. I heard a shriek and blood spattered everywhere. Ghosts, I thought.

I went up the stairs, the house was smelly, old and rotten. I got up the stairs and something pounced on me, it was a zombie. I shot, I missed. I only had one bullet left. I shot a rake on the wall and it fell on a zombie and killed it. William was still behind me, he hated violence. I suddenly saw something out of the corner of my eye, it was Paddy Pat, the Dark Avenger. Will and me had to take Paddy on. He tried to use his laser against us, we dodged it. We jumped and karate-kicked him and Will shot Paddy. Paddy was dead, Will started crying, but we were safe.

Tom Howard (10)
Westfield Junior School